&

Other Stories

KEPRESSNG

Ogu & Other Stories

KEPRESSNG

NIGERIA | UK

First Published in 2021

A catalogue record for this book is available from the British Library.
A catalogue record for this book is available from the National Library of Nigeria.

Cover design & illustrations by Chimele Ezinwo of Chigirl Arts & Design

978 978 999 280 5 (Hardback)
978 191 637 106 4 (Paperback)
978 191 637 107 1(Ebook)
978 978 999 281 2(Ebook)

INTRODUCTION

Kepressng (KEP) Ltd is an African publishing company with a vision that extends beyond just publishing. Our goal is to amplify the voice and power of African literary works and bring them to global recognition. We aim to shatter the myths that suggest Africans aren't readers and remind the world that our thirst for knowledge, stories, and culture is boundless. We stand firmly against the false notion that African literature is overlooked or undervalued, and we are determined to change that narrative.

Our core values are: **Excellence, Collaboration**, **Discovery & Generosity**.

At **KepressNG Ltd**, we believe that literature is not just about books - it's about preserving and sharing the essence of who we are as Africans. Through our initiatives, we aim to foster a global appreciation of African culture, history, and experiences, all while empowering our communities to take pride in their literary traditions.

THE NOTE

The theme of this competition was FESTIVE.
I feel we've judged our youths quite harshly in the past. They have so much to offer. We've seen that in their entries.
The stories reminded us that no one is perfect and that we'll always need someone. This is true for the maiden edition of this competition because people are generally wary of getting involved in things they know nothing about. We had not expected the number of entries that came in, and we're grateful for being given a chance.
There were other themes vested in our competition theme, and we will like to use this opportunity to thank the judges (one has chosen to remain anonymous)
Our Judges are:

1. Her Royal Highness, Mrs Louisa Ezinwo, former Civil Servant. She has worked with the Rivers State Civil Service for over twenty years in the education sector. In her free time, she works with several NGOs and rotates her travels around her numerous grandchildren.
2. Olukorede S. Yishau is an award-winning and widely-travelled Nigerian journalist, novelist and short-story writer. His first novel, *In the Name of Our Father*, was nominated for the Nigeria Prize for Literature. The novel has been a subject of theses by students in Nigerian universities. It was published by Parrésia Publishers Limited in 2018 and described by two-time Booker finalist Chigozie Obioma as a 'work of deceptive simplicity'. His collection of short stories *Vaults of Secrets* was released on October 1st, 2020. His poems were published in an anthology of poetry ACTIVISTS POETS. His essays and short stories have appeared in different publications. Yishau holds a degree in Mass Communications from Ambrose Alli University, Ekpoma, Edo State, Nigeria, as well as a professional diploma in Public Relations. He is one of four Nigerians nominated by the United States Mission in Nigeria for the University of Iowa creative writing programme on public health.
3. Last and not least is Kemka Ezinwo, better known as Agnes Kay-E, the bestselling author of Blossom in winter. She is also the creator of Kemka Ezinwo Press. Her ultimate ambition is to make African Literature legendary.

To

All who celebrate African literature.

To all the authors who made this possible.

TABLE OF CONTENT

The KepressNG Anthology Prize 2021 Shortlisted Stories

Bonus Stories

Miscellaenous

KEPRESSNG PRIZE 2021 Shortlisted stories

OGU

Mary-Ella E.

The hassles and bustles of the people of Rumuoyi village were at its peak in preparation for Ogu - the festival of a year's transition; its people were everywhere taking old stuff out of their huts or taking new things in - as was the tradition. It was the busiest day in Rumuoyi village. At midnight of the last day of the year, old things are taken to Esezi in the heart of the village, and everyone would, at the cusp of dawn, surround their old things in a large bonfire and chant the old saying:

'Year young, year old,
last day, last day
go with your troubles,
go with the past,
go with our pains.
stay with our past.

The drummers worked the song into a frenzy as they danced around the fire as it engulfed the things of the past year. It was believed to take the past pains with the dying fire. This began the Ogu festival. The following day, the dawn of the new year, they'd all return for the dance with the Ogu drum.

Nkasi-obi, a woman past her prime, dusted a beautiful velvet trouser suit that was laid out on her mattress with a dusting rag and smiled. She had practically cried her husband-to-be into paying for the all-too-expensive suit her husband-to-be had complained but still, come succumbed to her demands. He wasn't rich or anything, so the suit wasn't what he had wanted to use the salary he had worked so hard for.

Admiring her suit, she smiled once more. It was almost time; she looked at her husband-to-be's watch on the desk beside her.

Wait till they see me. They'll know my future husband is from the city, especially that stupid Mbechi. Mbechi had been a rival from childhood. Anything Nkasi-obi got, Mbechi got a better version of it, but not this, not him, not her Chibuike.

She smiled contently.

"Eleven forty-two," she thought aloud.

By then, the villagers were all at Esezi; some sitting, some standing, chitter-chatter from every open corner - everyone was happy. Nkasi-obi had finished getting dressed, her husband-to-be was relieved and gave her several compliments.

"Although you stress me out sometimes, my love for you will never be stressed," Chibuike finally said - It was practically his mantra for her.

Nkasi-obi smiled at him.

They hugged and were startled by the eruption of voices, and the heating of metal tins, raising a cacophony of various echoes around them. They smiled knowingly at each other and joined the cheer.

"Happy new year," they chorused as neighbours greeted neighbours, people hailed each other, admiring and dissenting their outfits, weather and hopes.

The Otu-Elulu eulogised the families, from their ancestors to the newest born. That family danced around him until he finished and moved to the next family to do the same, and they'd react the same way. When everyone had processed to Esezi, the drummers went to their designated spot at the Ogu drum.

The Ogu drums were stacked in a rack of steps with the biggest at the bottom; what held them together was a mystery to all except the drummers; even the selection of the drummers was a mystery. It was a thing of envy to play the drums and beyond beauty to listen to. These drums were raised in secret and on only three occasions: the death of the Nyeweli, Ogu Festival, in times of war. The drums were the major tourist attraction for Rumuoyi.

Nkasi-obi watched the dancers from neighbouring villages sweat and laugh, the fire dancers play with fire as if it was nothing, the masquerades chased children and young women, the array of assorted food on the tables spread wide enough to feed a nation, the elders whispering amongst themselves, then the Nyeweli dance into Esezi all his glory with his wives forming an emblem around him, soon after that Onye-Ozi'agbara with his minions hovering around and over him as he marched to the heart of Esezi.

Nkasi-obi's joy wasn't from the excitement that came with greeting the new year. It wasn't from the celebration or the splendid view. It was the fact that she had just gotten engaged, and the thought of it alone summoned butterflies in her stomach.

After so many years.

Nkasi-obi chuckled and sighed.

Finally, a bride I will be.

Nkasi-obi eyed her soon-to-be husband and smiled just as her stomach complained loudly.

Chibuike tried to disguise a laugh as he wrinkled his face, staring at her stomach.

"Let me just visit the food table for a second," Nkasi-obi mumbled. "Need anything?"

Chibuike shook his head in reply.

Nkasi-obi went towards the serving women but stopped dead in her tracks when she saw Mbechi and then made a full 360 degrees turn.

"Not now abeg," Nkasi-obi whispered to herself. Remembering the suit, she had put on for display, she turned right back and continued her strut towards the massive table.

Mbechi, who was at the large table and pouring herself a drink, tilted her head, and with a small smile, drawled, "Oh, is that Nkasi I see? Nkasi-obi?"

"It's me o!" Nkasi-obi retorted dryly as she picked a flat earthenware bowl and handed it to one of the serving women.

"I would say you don't look a day over fifty, but I'd be lying," Mbechi muttered and tried to get something out of her teeth.

Upset, Nkasi-obi pursed her lips. She exhaled and concentrated on the woman who was serving her but couldn't hold her tongue. "At least, I'm still beautiful enough to earn this outfit from my husband."

Mbechi smirked. "No outfit is enough to hide those wrinkles. And please, don't be silly. He's not your husband yet. You people haven't even done your traditional wedding." She laughed loudly, drawing the attention of the people nearby. "He's just looking for one of these young maidens to marry o! With you, he's just buying himself time, and time is what you don't have, my dear."

Nkasi-obi fumed and spat, "How dare you talk to me in that manner?"

"My dear, you're still a 'miss', and I am a 'Mrs', expecting another one soon too." Mbechi sneered, rubbing her swollen belly. "So, we are not mates."

Nkasi-obi watched Mbechi take out a serviette to wipe her hands and mouth and wrinkled her nose when Mbechi burped.

Mbechi made to leave, dropped her serviette in Nkasi-obi's food then covered her mouth in fake surprise. "Oops! Being pregnant sure makes you clumsy."

"Mbechi," Nkaso-obi cried.

Mbechi flicked her hair at her and hummed as she waltzed away.

Nkasi-obi pulled her back by the hair. "Don't

ever in your life speak to me like that or I will injure you."

Mbechi stared blankly at Nkaso-obi, then picked a knife from the table and thrust it at Nkasi-obi. Nkasi-obi had expected Mbechi's action, but it had happened so fast that there were two slits on the side of her suit.

Beyond anger and pain, Nkasi-obi pounced on Mbechi and beat her all the way to the centre of the celebration. The drummers stopped abruptly, making their fight more obvious to the large crowd. A mixture of shock, amusement and disgust were on the faces in the crowd as Nkasi-obi made an attempt to fill a pregnant woman's mouth with sand. The Nyeweli's guards intervened and took them away.

Nkasi-obi was put in a separate room because Mbechi was *afraid* of staying in the same room with a *madwoman* who beats up 'pregnant women'. She could see the door to the chamber room of the elders, and she could also see her husband-to-be, alongside a woman she could recognise from a mile away, her soon-to-be mother-in-law. They were judging her case. She had broken two rules:

'You can't lay your hands on a pregnant woman.' – it's a taboo.

'You can never and should never fight in Esezi, especially on market days and special occasions such as Ogu' – it's forbidden.

Nkasi-obi prayed silently that the judgement

wouldn't be harsh or expensive. A while later, a guard came to get her. The elders had given their verdict: a chicken, a goat, a few hot drinks and a fine for the treatment of the pregnant woman. She tried not to roll her eyes as no fine was given to Mbechi.

Annoyed, Nkasi-obi's father cut down the requirement of the bride price so she could leave the village at once. When they got to the car, her mother-in-law started lamenting.

"Look at the shame!!!" Nkasi-obi's mother-in-law started. "The disgrace! Never ever have we had a case like this to settle. Not in this family. Not in *my* family," her mother-in-law spat, then turned menacing eyes to Nkasi-obi, who lowered her gaze.

She stared at the two slashes on the suit and the dirt; the suit was barely recognisable. She had wanted it so badly, to impress everyone so badly. It had cost a fortune.

Oh! I showed off alright!

Chibuike drove, his mother beside him, Nkasi-obi in the back like a reject.

"God is showing this boy a sign, and he is turning a blind eye," Nkasi-obi's mother-in-law sighed woefully. "God is telling you not to go through with this! What are the odds that on Ogu, something like this, which has never happened, if I may add, has happened?"

Nkasi-obi's mother-in-law sighed, moaned, and continued in her woeful opinions and pining, while Nkasi-obi looked outside, and Chibuike drove the car carefully, face emotionless, staring straight ahead, without a word uttered except when stole glances at Nkasi-obi and winked or smiled at her. As soon as the car came to a halt at Chibuike's house in the city, Nkasi-obi's mother-in-law went into the house with arms flailing and blaming her late husband for leaving her to do a man's job.

Nkasi-obi, still ashamed, climbed out of the car with her head down and walked into the house and sat in the darker part of the parlour. She was expecting 'anything' at this point; his yelling would be the highest point of her stress, but she would take it. It was her fault for walking into Mbechi's trap.

Chibuike watched Nkasi-obi go into the house and exhaled heavily. He climbed out of his car, brought out Nkasi-obi's suitcases and locked the car. He went straight to his bedroom and didn't find her. He finally found her in the parlour. His mother was beside her, chewing cashew nuts and began to moan her existence when she saw him. He ignored his mother and went to Nkasi-obi, slipped his hands in hers and pulled her up, then guided her to their room, where he wiped her eyes of any evidence of tears.

"I'm always the last. In school, I was the last to get picked, in my grades, in buying anything, for school fees even," she sobbed.

Chibuike held her when she burst into tears.

"In the university, I just barely got out, and Mbechi was always there to remind me of what I didn't have," Nkasi-obi paused, then continued, "Things changed when I moved out of this village. I got a good job, but then I was old, or old-er. The villagers made it their duty to remind me every day. No one took that duty more seriously than Mbechi."

Chibuike rubbed her back, urging her to go on.

"Seeing her today reminded me of all those memories, of every time my mother would call me a bad omen, and I lost it. I let it get the best of me. I disappointed everyone, disappointed myself, proving the things that my mother said," Nkasi-obi sniffed and wiped her eyes. "Maybe your mother was right."

Chibuike cupped her face and raised it, so he could look into her eyes.

"I don't know who said all those things to you, but I guess they're the ones with the bad luck. Ever since I met you, you've been the only good thing. My good luck charm and my happiness. Only your stress that used to tire me." Chibuike grinned, smoothing the cheeks with the back of his hands. "Although you stress me out sometimes, my love for you will never be stressed."

Nkasi-obi smiled. A smile of relief, of love. She now believed his love was true.

"That girl will see you next time and head for

the hills. You fight like a mad person."

They laughed.

"You really like mad people o," Nkasi-obi mocked.

"So, you even know sey you mad sef," Chibuike jested.

"I can't wait for the next Ogu festival," Nkasi-obi said.

"Ha! We just entered a new year, my dear, relax! But hopefully, next year, you'll be the next pregnant woman, not the one that beat them up," Chibuike said, smiling.

"Will you ever let me live this down?" Nkasi-obi asked, wrinkling her face.

"Never o! We'll even name our first child Ogu," Chibuike blurted out, laughing, Nkasi-obi she joined him while attempting to use the pillow to swat him, and he covered his face in defence.

Mary-Ella E. is a Biochemistry undergraduate and hopes to remind women of the strength they have within them through writing. She loves reading and spends most of her free time as a photographer and makeup artist.

THE UNFORGETTABLE CHRISTMAS

Iquo Inyang

The war between Nigeria and Biafra had just ended. Everyone who had run away from Port Harcourt to Owerri and Umuahia were beginning to find their way back. Port Harcourt was a woeful scene of houses without roofs or partial roofing and mostly no windows or doors, walls filled with holes, bullets, and debris. Wherever you could excavate debris, and mortal remains became yours for a dwelling. There was no real source of right and wrong; people grabbed and secured whatever they could.

Mama secured a good-sized building with two bedrooms on the ground floor plus a garage. The upper floor was empty and with barely any walls left. It was enough for our family of six girls and two boys.

Hunger abounded.

Uzonwane, the Ada of the house, was a go-getter; she did the 'attack market' during the war and joined the Win the War Caritas and then the Red Cross Movement after the war. This

movement came with weekly supplies of provisions and condiments for food; there was no money anywhere.

Mama also, in her wisdom, became a distributor to the only existing retail outlet, UAC (United African Company). The garage of the house became a store to sell most of these items. The house was overly full, with four older sisters, and the next thing to do was, as Mama put it, 'at your age, I was married to your father'.

This pressure for marriage was so intense that it was an obvious palpitation in all of us. On me, because my sisters would pick on me. Even Igwe, my elder brother, because he always took Mama's side of the argument. This trepidation became part of us on the way home from the sales of whatever was our chore for the day. Like a prayer answered, all but two of my sisters, the first and last two, that is, got married within a year. Unfortunately, my most annoying sister, Uzonwanne, wasn't one of them.

The state government finally found its feet and started proper governing. New laws came. One of which was about the occupancy of seemingly abandoned houses. One had to pay or purchase from the government. It was very political, and schemers schemed us out of our home.

We were left with one option: go to the village. We were not pleased with heading for the village. It took some getting used to. By the end of the week, life in the village became seamless.

Although it was harmattan season, the weather was dry and scorched, so we ended our day with a wash in the stream. We learned how to dive after gulping water through our noses. We learned how to roast corn, pear, catch falling udala, and climb an orange tree without breaking its fragile branches. At night, we joined the gatherings for tales by moonlight.

Mama was uncomfortable with our relationship with the villagers, but she soon let us be. The freedom lasted only two days because she started a *mama-put* centre the following day and being the only boy in the house, I was expected to greet customers. Mama specialised in bushmeat, fresh fish pepper soup and nkwaobi.

I began to notice that Mama was sad. She was not only sad, but she was also lonely. There were no telephones and then the letters never came. Igwe, my elder brother, had been sent abroad with the dowries from Eziuzo, Ezinne, Ugwe. Uwa's dowry, which was supposed to be saved for me, had been used to take us to the village.

Mama would count the money she'd earned at the end of the day and sigh. She would raise it over her head with open arms and put it in a tin box and tuck it under her bamboo bed. I still wondered how Mama could sleep on that hard bed and not feel pain, like us. One day, I heard Mama talk to herself, 'one naira for… five naira…. How will I get bushmeat for tomorrow…" then Mama walked up and down, and you could hear her because she scrubbed the ground with one leg - that was how we knew Mama was still awake.

One day, I was called aside by a man who had come with a few friends. He had money because he paid for everybody's food and beer. The man wanted to speak to my sister, Uzonwanne, the annoying one. He was going to pay me two hundred naira just to speak to my sister.

I couldn't believe my annoying sister could be useful for something. If I get my sister to him, she could marry him. I'll have peace, and I'll still have two hundred naira so that we can eat chicken with rice and stew on Christmas Day. Also, Mama won't need to work on Christmas Day, which was over eight days away.

It was a good idea, I agreed. Knowing how annoying Uzonwane could be, I didn't tell her why I needed her help. But as soon as the man gave me the money he shouted:

"Take her!"

"Ewo'o!" I exclaimed and shouted: "Headhunters!" Then something hit the back of my head, and I fell. When I woke up, we were in a tiny hut. Everyone in it was covered in mud, including my annoying sister. The man closest to the door was tied up; he looked mad because saliva dripped from both sides of his mouth, and he bared his teeth.

Uzonwanne, my annoying sister, eyed me.

"I didn't know o! He just told me he wanted to speak to you."

"How much did he pay you?"

"Two hundred naira."

"Stupid boy."

We heard: 'kaboom' twice. We ducked and covered our heads with our hands.

"What is happen outside?" a woman cried.

"I don't know o," a gruff voice responded. "But I smell goatmeat, and I am hungry."

I looked at the mad man and swallowed spit. My annoying sister smelt of goatmeat; she was still cooking it when I called her.

"This is your fault and your longer throat," My annoying sister said and hissed. "If I lose my chance of getting married tomorrow, I'll kill you and bury you, and our mother will never be able to find your body."

I believed her. Even though I didn't understand the talk of getting married, my annoying sister has never been known to say anything she didn't mean. Also, she was strong like a man. I swallowed. I now understood why Mama made me use lime to clean the rust on her George wrappers; I didn't know she was getting married.

"Fire!" a voice shouted from outside. Other voices followed.

"Where them?" a voice shouted from outside, and something crashed. A few minutes passed, and the door of the hut they were in fell in, and a man danced in with a shining cutlass in his hand. He took my annoying sister's hand, and I

shouted.

"Ey leave her o! Take me instead."

The man sneered at me and asked, "Why?"

"Please don't use my sister for rituals."

The man with the cutlass grimaced and turned his head and shouted, "Are they complete?"

"How did you find us?" My annoying sister asked the man who was now loosening the rope around her wrist.

"Uzọ̀'s *ashewo,* the one with one eye and walks funny." the man said and lifted my sister and stared down at me. "She directed us."

I was afraid to ask why he kept an eye on me.

"And it took this long?" my annoying sister asked.

I was expecting her to be happy.

"What if I was already cooking inside somebody's pot?"

I agreed with her. I swallowed spit before I could parrot and remind them by my presence that I was the one who put us in this mess.

"This is a forest. And I did not know you were missing," the man snapped.

My annoying sister stared coldly at me and mouthed, "I will deal with you later," then nodded. As if that wasn't enough, she folded her hands, ready to punch me. I shifted from her and steadily watched her hands.

"Let us go before their main Oga comes to waste us."

Waste us?

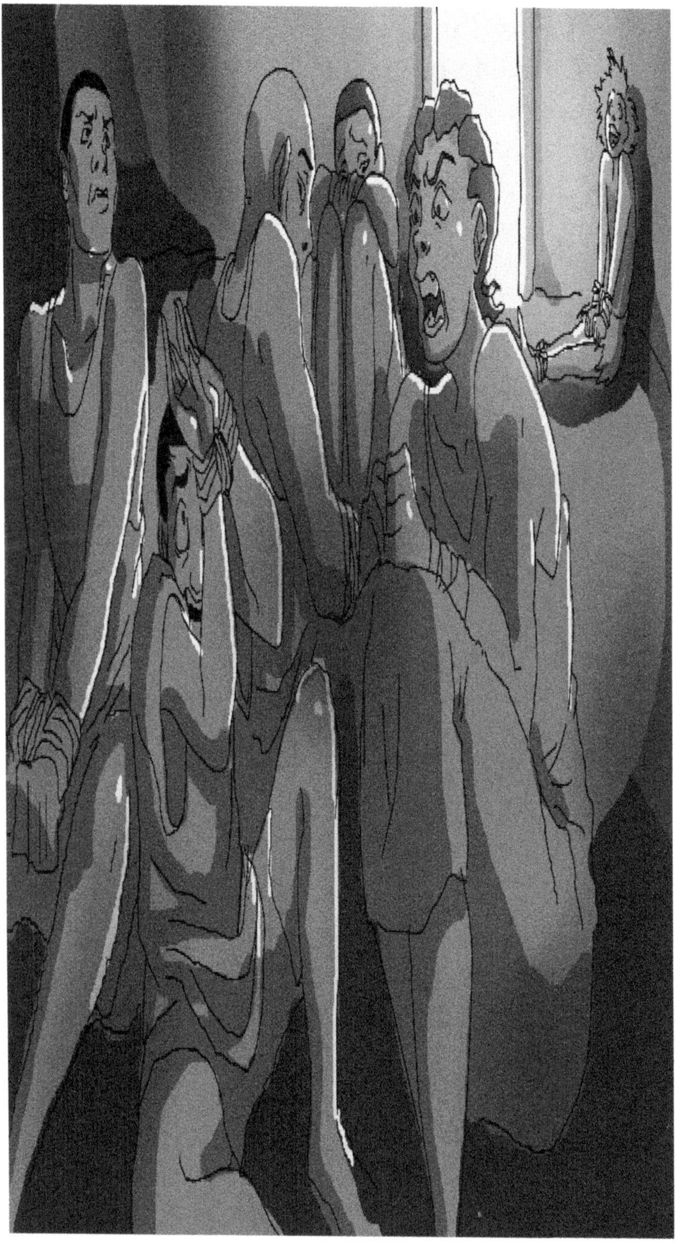

"Waste us?" my annoying sister asked.

"This people no be head hunter o! Them dey chop people."

"Ewe'eeee!" I cried out and placed my hands on my head. I could see thick dark clouds of smoke in my mind. I could imagine an oversized pot with my head dancing on top of it and people laughing as it sunk to the bottom of the pot.

"Ngwa nu!" another man joined us with a few more mud-covered people.

They took us home safely. Uzonwanne, my annoying sister, got married the following day and didn't get to pound me as she had promised. But Mama made sure I was the only one breaking palm kernel for its nuts until it was time for school, and then she sent me off to boarding school.

Iquo Inyang is a retired civil servant and is curious about the human mind. She enjoys travelling, reading and speech writing.

BEYOND THIS RAGING BEACH

John Otroyin

Sleep is never enough when you are woken up forcefully with a dirty slap. I lifted my head from the floor and saw Màmá staring down at me with a frown. I needed not be reminded it was a Tuesday morning and must go to the beach to receive Bàbá. Ọmọlará slapped my head again. She thought I'd drifted back to sleep, but I was booting and trying to calm the sharp ring in my head. I got up with borrowed strength to challenge her; Màmá would not have it. She flashed me a sour look, and I halted in my track, wearing a contorted face as I gnashed at my twin sister. I folded my sleeping mat and marched out with heavy strides at Màmá's command.

Outside the hut, I washed my face from the water pot and peed by Ìyáàgbà's grave, rushing through, for Màmá disapproved of peeing on the grave. I made circles on the ugly epitaph with my urine, and nostalgia hit me. Ìyáàgbà's stories and her cooking crowded my thoughts. I remembered vividly one of her many stories—the one about the giant snake.

This was before Bàbá stopped talking; before brother Ọ̀sàdáre and brother Ọ̀sàdípẹ̀ left. Long ago, she narrated, when the people of Orímẹdú freshly settled on the land near the beach, after a long migration, a large snake lived on the beach. The people offered sacrifices to the benevolent snake, and it left the land to make the sea its home.

From then on, some families started worshipping the snake, and in return, every three hundred years, the snake blessed one villager with wealth. When fishing, once a man pulls out his net and finds the head of the snake, Ìyáàgbà said, he is automatically wealthy. He becomes even more important than the village leader. My elder brothers followed Bàbá fishing the next morning, eager to be the favoured one. The twins were twelve then and had never spent the night in the sea. They just did what other boys did, which was to wait by the beach for arriving fishers,When I woke again to help pull the boat to shore, and to push new ones into the sea.

I felt another slap on the back of my head. Now outside, I was sure I would hit Ọmọlará with a heavy slap she won't forget anytime soon, but it was Màmá.

"What have I told you about peeing on your

granny's grave?" she quarrelled in Yorùbá with a low voice. Màmá's voice could be mistaken for a man's, and when she speaks with anger, it sounds an octave lower.

"No. I… the." I tried to lie, but my kiní was still above the band of my ṣòkòtò, so I sucked my teeth and went into the hut to grab a shirt. Then I walked to the beach behind Màmá, side eying Ọmọlará who was having a good time about my bad morning. She seemed to be after me in this life, and only my sadness brought her joy. This was not how brother Ọ̀ṣàdáre did with his twin brother, Ọ̀ṣàdípẹ̀, when they were still here. In fact, when they left, it was a planned arrangement, and they left together. I silently planned to get back at her as we walked to the beach, chewing my teeth.

Chilling sea breezes greeted us as we got to the few huts that led to the beach. Màmá walked in front with two plastic bowls under her left arm, while Ọmọlará followed right behind with a bag containing new clothes for Bàbá. I walked behind them till we got to the beach; Màmá joined other women who were also waiting for their husbands and fish dealers from big markets in the city eager to fill their bowls with fishes freshly seduced out of their habitat.

As Màmá greeted the other women, I went close to the beach and scanned the horizon for any trace of Bàbá. His boat wasn't among those trying to reach land, so I walked down toward the wrecked ship. Growing up, this ship used to be our playground, now it has become a public toilet. People squatted over with the ship's large metallic body as a shield and took shits, while tides washed the shit away into the ocean. I dug a shallow hole into the sand, pulled down my shorts, and bent over. Hardly had I started when I saw Bàbá's boat approaching.

Young men ran towards his boat after he successfully got his boat through the raging beach. When they finally pushed Bàbá's boat to the elevated white sand where the water wave couldn't reach, he brought out his catch. He nodded to our greeting, collected the bag from Ọmọlará, and went to the wrecked shit to change. When he left, Màmá emptied the sack into the sand, and we knelt around it.

Màmá shook her head pensively at the catch. It was barely more than half full; Bàbá, too, wasn't happy with his catch by the way he pulled his body like a bag of wet cement. You would know how much he worked all night long. We sorted the fishes into categories: fingerlings, medium, big, and special species. Immediately after the sorting was done, the traders would pick the ones they wanted and pay cash for the goods (usually the big ones which they took to their cold rooms in the market). Then, we would fill our bowls with the fingerlings, which we would cook with smoke and then sell in the local market.

Bàbá returned in his new clothes when we had almost finished sorting the fishes. He gave me a cold look, and I caught myself. He always discouraged me from sorting the fish; he made me understand that it was a job for women and boys should either be fishing or helping fishers land their boats. He pointed to a group of boys pulling a boat to shore, and I knew he wanted me to join them. I slowly left the sorting spot with a bowed head and walked as if towards the group of men battling with the boat. When Bàbá turned around, I scurried to the ship to continue my shit.

I saw a figure walking up and thought it was another boy coming to empty his stomach, but when the image grew closer, I noticed it was the daughter of the Chief, Ìdòwú.

Ìdòwú was the tenth daughter of the wicked Chief – he had so many sons nobody bothered to count. I sprang up, pulled my pants, dropped my shirt, and frantically covered the hole with sand. I stood there looking into the large expanse of the sea as she passed, convincing myself that I was just brooding there, but who was I fooling? She knew already what people came here to do. Why did she have a smirk on her face, and why did she pass here? I made sure she was well out of sight before I dug a fresh hole and poured the content of my stomach that was threatening to sabotage me.

I was enjoying the dance group's practice by the shrine that evening. Although I longed to, I never tried to join them because Bàbá disapproved of things like this. The group was choreographing the water dance. The dancers – eight of them – were lined in rows of two. The drummers started their instrument slowly, then gradually, they increased the tempo, hitting sticks on their drums dexterously as if the sticks were an extension of their hands. Dancing on the spot, the dancers worked more with their hands and the upper trunk, for on the festival day, they would be dancing in the sea, and only these parts would be visible. I was totally lost in the beautiful art when Àjàlá passed by and asked why I was with the dance group when a furore was garnering mass in my father's house. I ran as fast as my short legs could carry me.

We lived inland, close to the farmlands that lead to nowhere. When I got home, Bàbá was on the floor; the clothes he wore had sand all over like a kid that rolled in the mud. The wicked Chief was in his notorious all-white agbádá, and his boys stood behind him, their shorts stained as if they'd just wrestled with catching a stray cow that was eating vegetables from a farm. Màmá knelt beside Bàbá, her hands clasped and raised above her head. Chief Olórímẹ́wàá spoke slowly as if counting his Yorùbá.

"I will return the day after the water festival. May the gods help you raise my money by then, if not." He raised his eyes to my twin sister, who was hugging the doorframe of our hut. "I will take her as payment. I have tried enough." With those words, he pushed his protuberant stomach in front, and his men followed gingerly behind like flies behind someone who'd just taken a shit and didn't wash.

As soon as the Chief turned around, the crowd dispelled. For about two minutes, Bàbá crouched on the spot, thinking, then got up, dusted sand off his body, got a hoe, and left for the farm. Màmá called after him, but he didn't turn. Màmá scolded me for my absence before she entered the kitchen to start dinner.

Bàbá entered the house just when the fowl were singing their morning chorus. He'd worked all night on the farm. Màmá and Ọmọlará too woke up. The morning light was not sufficient, so Màmá asked me to put on the àtùpà, but Bàbá protested with a no sound and asked us to sleep by putting clasped hands under his chin and tilting his head.

When I woke again, morning light had filled our hut. I got up and started preparing for the farm, but Bàbá asked me to carry the ewédú he'd harvested over the night to our ewédú customer. The leaves were yet to mature, but I obeyed. After washing and eating, I took the commodity to the buyers: the Àjàní family. They lived by the beach, so after delivering, I took a walk to the beach to take a quick shit by the ship.

Some boys were playing football, and a crowd had gathered to watch. After emptying my bowels, I joined the spectators. If Bàbá caught me, he would squeeze my ears and lift me off the ground so that when he dropped me, my ears would have a terrible burning sensation. Then Màmá would speak for him that only jobless and lazy people indulged in things like this.

Bàbá and Màmá worked so much, but there is nothing to show for it. The little we had, we put into saving for Chief Olórímẹ́wàá. I wondered exactly how much Bàbá owed him. Surely, Bàbá wouldn't watch him take Ọmọlará for one of his wives. He had so many of them, which he treated like fish bones. One of the players kicked the ball into the makeshift goalpost, and the crowd erupted. Other boys ran around the scorer, and women gyrated, shaking their buttocks with glee. I never understood the spirit that possessed these ball people, and I didn't like the game.

As I walked away from the gleeful lunatics, Ìdòwú called behind me. I turned, and she ran up. I straightened my shirt and noticed I'd left home without my flip-flops. I cursed under my breath and focused on trying to smile.

"Hello Ọmọ́jọlá," she greeted with a smile, and I responded, trying to imitate her sweet Yorùbá.

She asked where I was headed. I told her I was going home, and she offered to escort me. We talked as we walked. When we got to the last group of huts by the beach, she pulled me to the back of an abandoned hut – it used to belong to Sojí, the madman, but he had disappeared the year before. Ìdòwú pulled down my shorts and took my kiní into her hands, all the while looking into my eyes.

My heart did plenty of somersaulting in my chest, but I didn't stop her. I didn't want to. She went down on one knee and pushed my back against the hut. Barely had she started when someone saw us. He walked up and landed a heavy slap on my face but didn't touch Ìdòwú. He just commanded us to disappear.

When I got home, Bàbá asked for the money

for the ewédú I went to deliver. I dipped my hand into my pocket and brought out nothing. Bàbá grew livid, and my ears tingled in anticipation of the inevitable. When Bàbá raised me by my squeezed ears and dropped me, I felt the ears were still attached to his hands. He went in and returned with a pankéré. After lashing every part of my body with the unbreakable cane, he ordered me to sleep. Despite the preceding violence, I dreamed of beautiful things.

I dreamed of Ìyáàgbà, and her èfó-rírò, and her stories.

I dreamt of Ìdòwú on a beautiful farm filled with young maize plants. It was our wedding ceremony, and we were about to kiss to the cheering of a small crowd when Ọmọlará slap my head. I woke up with a frown and a tight pain in my buttocks. Bàbá was leaving for the sea. He ordered me to join him. Immediately, dread replaced my body pains. My brothers, too, were twelve when they went on their first fishing experience, but Ìyáàgbà's tale gingered them, and that was four years ago. I hated the water, and even though I was a good swimmer, I felt that the sea hated me, and I always avoided it. Surely, this was my punishment for being careless with the ewédú money.

The walk to the beach that day was the longest. The evening was young, and the horizon above the sea seemed cheerful. Other fishers were prepping their boats, while some pushed theirs into the sea. Bàbá filled the engine with gas and inspected his fishing net. Baits were arranged in the net and tossed into the boat. While Bàbá prepped, I watched other fishermen take off into the sea. You must wait for a strong tide to wash to the shore, then you push the boat against the tide with the help of other young men. Once in the deep parts, you jump in and immediately start the engine. If you are cursed and your engine fails, you are left to the mercy of the ocean current, and like coconut, it will wash you to wherever. Unless you can swim, then you jump into the sea, swim to the shore, and chase your boat with a new one.

When Bàbá was ready for take-off, other boys joined in pushing the boat. Soon the boat left shallow water into the deeps, and Bàbá pulled the engine start, and we zoomed off into the eerie ambience of the sea. The beach and the people in it started reducing in size until it was out of sight. The sea is another world of its own with nothing but water, deafening breezes, cold, and the sky above it like an endless canopy.

Night fell on us, still travelling. We travelled for a few more hours before Bàbá turned off the engine of the boat. He took the paddle and stirred the water. The wave made the boat rock so badly I felt dizzy at once. Bàbá cast the net into the water and sat still in the boat, looking distant. He only stirred if an angry wave rocked the boat too hard, but we didn't go far from the cast net.

After a while, he pulled the net. We removed the catch into a sack, refilled the bait, cast, sat, and stirred the water when a heavy wave hit. The helpless fishes jostled in the boat, gasping frantically before resigning to fate. After some time, Bàbá started the engine, and we moved to another far spot, turned off the engine, and started the process again. I shivered as cold bit into my bones and marvelled at how Bàbá navigated the waters for every angle looked just like the last.

I didn't know when I fell asleep; it was the rain that woke me. When I raised my head and looked around, I could see the tiny outline of the beach. Soon we reached, and Bàbá turned off the engine and started paddling in no particular direction. The stupid raging beach again. Other returning fishers paddled, waiting patiently for a strong tide before pushing their boats through. When we got to shore, Màmá and Ọmọlará were already waiting. Màmá squeezed my hands when we greeted. She must have been worried sick. Ọmọlará too, there was genuine care in her eyes when she gave me dry clothes to change into. We sold the marketable fishes and carried the fingerlings home. When we got home, Màmá prepared a sumptuous fish stew which we ate with rice to celebrate my first fishing experience.

The water festival is a double feast for the Orímẹdú clan. It was on this same day that the water had allowed our ancestors to settle on this land long, long ago. It is a custom that everyone wears only white clothes. The rich men of the village wore draping agbádá like the Chief's uniform, while those who couldn't afford the exuberant cost of the lanky tailors—who claimed they paid through their noses to learn the trade from masters in the city who deprived them of touching the machine for years while they apprentices are preoccupied with bathing the children and doing menial jobs for the masters—wore ṣòkòtò and bùbá made from cheap materials.

But one couldn't tell class from the women's dressing, for even the poorest showed up in one of the best styles, properly adorned. Màmá wore the same ìró and bùbá she used the year before, Bàbá too. But Ọmọlará and I took pride in our new clothes made from sparkling satin material. We walked to the shrine from whence the procession to the beach would begin. After the prayer at the shrine, the procession started.

At the beach, I looked around for Ìdòwú. I wanted to show her my new clothes, and maybe we could sneak out to Sojí's abandoned hut. When I found her, she was on the laps of the same man that had separated us and dashed me a dirty slap. My stomach churned badly.

I felt betrayed.

I wanted to walk up to them and state my case, but I had none. He was taller and bigger; I was merely a dot on the floor and my short legs made me look like a six-year-old. He was a man with plenty of money to give to her, and I just started fishing only days ago. I felt a rumbling in my stomach at once. As the beach was full of people, shitting by the ship was impossible, so I ran home, allowing my tears to drop as I ran.

I cried while I shat. I had plans to marry Ìdòwú despite our families' feud. I had plans to take her to the city like my big twin brothers, and we would come back to Orímẹdú very rich. After I'd cried my eyes out, there was no interest to return to the festivity at the beach, so I went inside to rest my aching head.

Bàbá startled me when I entered the hut. I hadn't expected him to be in the house. I greeted and he waved back the greeting. He had many naira notes on one side of the bed and a few straightened ones on another. I covered the floor with my mat and pretended to be asleep. He looked pensive after counting the notes for the umpteenth time.

Surely, we were not prepared for the Chief's visit. The Chief didn't bluff. If his money wasn't ready, he would take my twin: this I couldn't bear. Thinking of the horror made my stomach churn again. I dashed to the back of the house and dug a hole to shit. After this, I went into the hut and slept.

I woke when Bàbá had left for the farm and Màmá was telling Ọmọlará something that made her weep—prepping her for marriage to the wicked Chief, maybe.

I got up and washed my face. The Chief would marry my sister over my dead body. I went in, fetched some baits, and left for the beach. I baited the nets, inspected the engine, and beckoned on a few boys to help push the boat into the evening waters. A heavy tide came at once, and there was no resistance. The beach forgot its rage. I had followed Bàbá fishing five more times by now, but that didn't explain why I wasn't scared of venturing into the sea by myself. There were no other fishers on the sea, just me and my stupid intuition.

When I felt like it, I stopped the engine and cast the net. There were no angry waves, but I brought out my paddle and stirred like Bàbá. After a while, I pulled the net with all my strength, removed the catch, and replaced the bait. I changed location arbitrarily and cast my net. It was at my fifth cast that I felt something too heavy to pull. When I used my last strength, the boat threatened to tumble, but I still pulled. Where had my fears gone to? I sat in the middle of the boat to catch my breath; then I started pulling. It was at this point I saw the head. Its head was as big as a cow's.

At once, I flung the net into the sea, then froze. The snake raised its head and dipped into the sea; its large body followed suit until its tail popped up and dipped back. I didn't know how I managed to, but I started the engine of the boat and zoomed away. It should be midnight when I arrived at the beach because no soul was in sight.

I was too busy running for my life that I forgot

to turn off the engine when I got to the beach, and the boat capsized with the wave. I fell into the water and swam quickly. The ocean tide made my swimming useless. When I realized this, I surrendered to the current and gently swayed up and down in obedience, waiting for a strong tide to wash me to the shore.

Ìyáàgbà's tales were true! The giant snake found me worthy; surely the sea wouldn't swallow me, I assured my spirit.

John Otroyin is a Nigerian BMW – Baritone, Marketer (social media), and a Writer. He is passionate about Opera and adores Jessye Norman. He is a finalist for Black Pheonix Inc and NHCP short story competitions. His works are published in the African Writers Magazine, Kansas State University's Touchstone, Praxis Magazine, Agbowó, AfroAnthologySeries, Kalahari Review, Light Post, and elsewhere. He holds a certificate of Creative writing from Wesleyan University, Connecticut (MOOC). He is an alumnus of Ake and Short Story Day Africa writing workshops. He writes from Lagos and lives online.

THE FESTIVAL OF HEADS

Testimony Odey

I have not been able to sleep since the head arrived. It seemed to carry some sort of demonic presence like it's waiting for the right time to strike. I imagine her name is Ada. It's dark outside, and a half-moon is the only source of light right now. Crickets sing. Owls howl. I sigh. I have been on the bamboo bed for the past hour, turning and breathing heavily. My body is wrapped in Mother's green wrapper, yet I shake from the cold. The weather had been hot and dry earlier in the day, grains of sand swirling in the air and clinging to bare feet.

Ugo, my elder sister, snores softly. Her short hair is plaited all black, and I think of how rough it is. She smiles, and I catch my breath. Mother had always said never to smile back when someone asleep smiled at you. I didn't dare ask why, although my curiosity was eating me up. When Ugo mumbles something in a quiet whisper, I am not sure of what she's saying. Her mouth twitches, and she mumbles again. I place my palms against my ears and close my eyes. I try to sleep and start by counting one to ten. I remain awake after the counting, and so, I take deep breaths, determined to count until I fall asleep. This time, I start from one, but I do not know the last number I whisper. All I know is that I am being drawn into a strange world of darkness.

The cockcrow wakes me up. At first, my head spins, and my eyes hurt. After a few minutes, the discomfort fades away, and I'm sitting on the bed. Ugo turns, and the bamboo bed makes a faint complaint. She has a very small smile on her lips, and her eyes are lightly closed, yet I know she is deeply asleep. She looks so peaceful, and I decide against waking her. I stand up from the bed; this time, it makes an audible sound that wakes Ugo. She yawns and stretches her hands above her head. Then she rubs her eyes and stares at me blankly.

"Good morning," I greet.

She nods. "How was the night?"

I shrug. She stands, and we both take our toothbrushes and distinct plastic cups and fetch water from the drum. I know everyone else is in their rooms because Ugo and I see nobody as we move outside. It's still dark, but I am sure in a short while, the sun will begin to rise.

While brushing, Ugo slightly hits my arm. I

moan, and she sticks her tongue out.

"The Festival of Heads is tomorrow," she says.

"Are you comfortable with Ada's head that Father brought home yesterday?" I ask.

"Who is Ada?"

"The girl whose head Father brought home."

Ugo raises her brow at me. I automatically know that she is asking how I knew the girl's name was Ada.

"I just made it up. She was a human. I just thought it would be honourable to give her a name."

Ugo laughs and shakes her head. I repeat the question I asked earlier.

"He had no choice."

For the second time, I shrug. He did have a choice. It wasn't mandatory that he participated in something so barbaric. If I were the one, I wouldn't be part of the Manly Men Association, but his ego needed to be pampered. Father joined the Manly Men Association, also referred to as MMA, last year. He couldn't hide his joy when he was asked to be a member. You see, you couldn't request to be a member of the MMA. The association picked their members, and it was considered one of the highest honours a man could get. Members of the association were participants in the Festival of Heads, along with the dancers and drummers.

The King would open the festival with prayers, and not too long after the Manly Men would showcase how many skulls they were able to get throughout the year. The man with the highest heads in his possession would be given eight plots of land and a huge amount of money.

"Are you listening to me?" Ugo asks.

I turn and shake my head. "What were you saying?"

"Can you help me make my hair today?"

I nod. Ugo would dance at the festival. Her wrappers and jewelleries were ready. I had seen her practice with the dancing team at the riverbank, and I had never been prouder of the way her waist shook rhythmically. When we get back into the house, Papa has his hoe and gun in his hands. Ugo and I kneel to greet him. He blesses us and goes out to the farm. Ugo takes a stool and sits in front of the house, losing her hair. I find Mother at the kitchen - a shed with a zinc roof - cutting yam into small cubes. I greet her, and she smiles and prays for me.

"Are you ready for the festival?

I sigh and nod. I have no choice.

"There's excitement in the air. I'll be going to

Mama Nneka's place this afternoon. We women will meet ourselves there."

They will pound yam until beads of sweat drop from their forehead, and they can barely lift their arms. They will wash meat and cook soups of different kinds with it. They will taste as they cook and later stand in small circles, talking about whose husband was richer.

"What are you thinking about?" Mother asks.

"The delicious food you will prepare when you go to Mama Nneka's place."

"Don't worry. I'll put some meat in my wrapper for my dear children," she says, and I laugh. It was Mother's usual practice - to steal pieces of meat and give to us. I slice the big green vegetables she will use for the porridge. Then I try to remove as many bones as I can from the dried fish. I am barely done when Mother snaps her finger as though remembering something.

"Has that your lazy brother gotten up from bed?" she asks.

"I don't know."

"I'm sure he's still on his bed, snoring away his destiny. Go and tell him that if he does not come outside and start doing something reasonable with his life, I will not take it easy with him. His mates have gone to the farm since morning,"

Mother hisses.

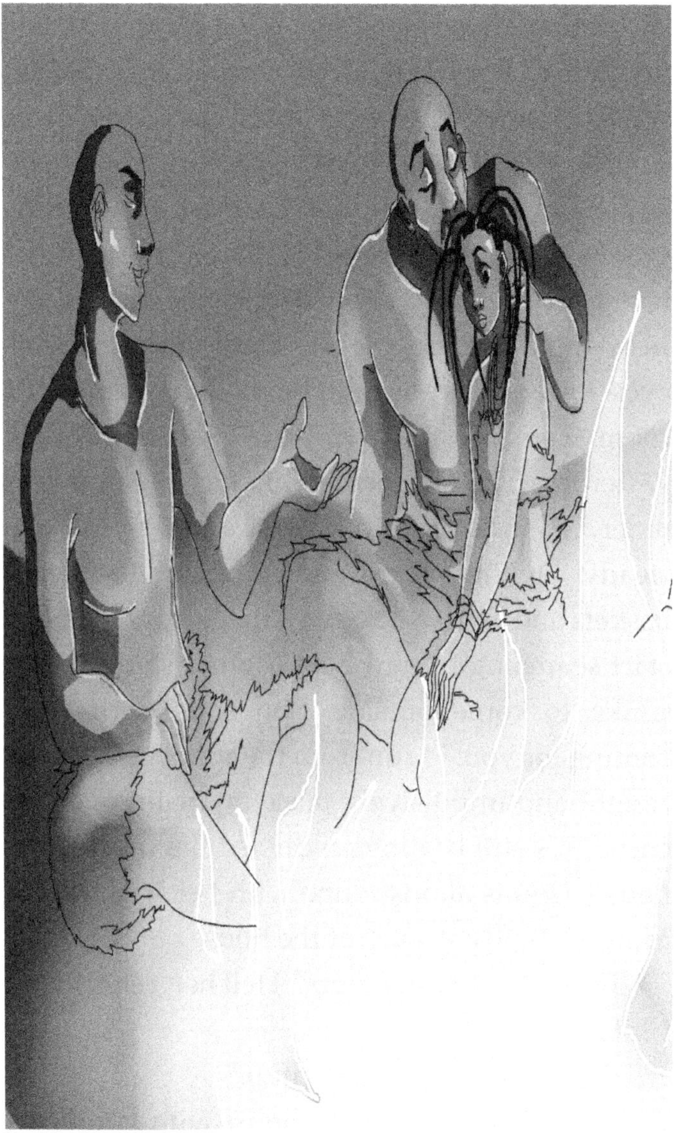

I find Chike on his bed like Mother had said.

He's the youngest in the house, as well as answers to Mother's prayers for a male child. Father's family had not taken it lightly when a male child was not coming on time. I tap Chike gently. He is snoring heavily and loudly, his legs wide open and a finger in his mouth. I tap harder until he groans and opens his eyes. I tell him what Mother had said that he better start doing something reasonable with his life. He hisses and closes his eyes. I leave his room and move into my parent's room, looking for the head Father brought yesterday. The girl seemed like my age or a year older. My heart beats heavily, and I try to take steady breaths. They are so many bags and baskets and calabashes, and I'm not sure where to start searching from. I hear Mother shouting for Chike to come outside. She ends with, "I'm coming for you." I run from the room before I am caught and impulsively place my palm over my chest - it's still beating wildly. At the front of the house, Ugo is almost done with her hair. I meet Mother at the entrance of the house.

"He refused to stand up," I tell her, referring to Chike.

"I'm already coming for him."

I watch her walk into the house with a purpose, a purpose that will end up moving Chike to tears.

Ugo motions for me to come.

"I'm done losing it. Come and help me weave it. What hairstyle do you think will fit me?"

I tell her every hairstyle looks good on her. She is not satisfied with the answer. I come to the conclusion of plaiting bucket style for her. When I am done, she admires the hair and gives me a brief hug. We eat breakfast while Chike goes to deliver Father's food to him on the farm. He grumbled and frowned when Mother asked him to help Father on the farm - a frown that had caused Mother to knock his head.

I was left at home alone. Chike had gone to the farm, Mother to Mama Nneka's place, and Ugo to the final dance practise with her friends. I used the opportunity to check out Father's room, to search for the head of Ada. There is a smaller room in my parent's room, a room that no one dares enter, not even my mother. I did not know why but Father had strongly warned us against it. I ignore the wild beating of my heart and go into the smaller room. It smells of dead, decaying things, and I hold my breath for a second. I find it in a small, woven basket. There is a bigger basket with so many other heads, heads of strangers who were not from the village. The room is gloom; the only source of light coming from the bigger room.

I move the small basket out into the sunlight. Her hair is plaited in tight and neat rows. Her eyes are opened, wide open, bulging. Her mouth hangs in a small O-shape, and I shiver.

How could Father?

He didn't even bother to close her eyes. She is dark; her skin still has a kind of glow in it. I want to run my fingers over her pointed nose and rub my thumb across her cheeks, petting her to sleep. I want to loosen her hair, re-weave it and tell her everything is going to be alright. I want to carry her head with my hands and lift them to the sun and breathe life into her nostrils. I take the basket back to the smaller room.

The next morning, everyone mumbles greetings and gets going. Chike sneaks out of the house like a thief, no doubt to see his friends. Ugo goes to see her friends. She is adorned with bangles, anklets, and waist beads. She looks so happy and excited. Mother goes to help the women in the final food preparation. Father goes for an early morning meeting with the Association of Manly Men. We all have an unspoken rule - to meet ourselves in the market square by five in the evening. While everyone is gone, I sweep the compound and put the house in order.

We will meet at the market square by five. The festival starts off with opening prayers by the King as usual. After that, the drummers come out, beating their drums in a way that makes the King take his Queen's hands and begin to dance. Some married men and their wives do the same.

After the drumming, hefty young men emerge to wrestle. There are chants leading them on. I look away to Chike. He is climbing the mango tree at the left end of the market, his friends sitting on the branches. He looks at me, a silly smile in his eyes. Ugo runs her hands through her hair. I can tell she is extremely nervous.

Father sits with members of the Manly Men. They whisper something between themselves and can't stop laughing. Mother is among other women serving garden eggs and groundnuts. The main meal will come later after the contest of the man possessing the highest number of heads has been held. The dancers come in. Ugo is the one who leads the other maidens, and they start by waist-breaking. There are loud cheers from the crowd, louder than the ones that erupted during the wrestling matches. My eyes are fixed on Ugo alone. I am pleased with her dancing skills. Soon, members of the Manly Men move to the stage. They have baskets in front of them, and they smile.

This is the very reason for the celebration. The men bring out the heads in their basket, the crowd keeping a record of the amount they have taken out so far. There are seven members of the Manly Men, including Father. When it reaches his turn, he keeps stretching his hands forth, bringing out more and more heads which causes a loud shout of encouragement from the crowd. Something strange runs down my spine when he brings out Ada's head. I look at her head, dumped among so many others. I don't know if I am just imagining it, but she winks at me. My body stiffens and I look at her again.

Nothing strange happens, and I am relieved.

After some minutes, it is clear that the winner is father. He jumps up in joy, and I see Mother dance in circles. Applauds and whistles fill the air. Two wrestlers lift Father up and sit him on their shoulders. Children are running around, laughing, and pointing at the heads on the ground. There are others mumbling, dissatisfied at the outcome of the contest. After Father had been carried to and fro for people to see and hail him, he was dropped on the floor. Then, the serving of pounded yam and various soups starts. After everyone has wined and dined, I go to see

Father. I whisper a soft *congratulation* as expected of me. I greet the rest of the Manly Men. Nnoja, a Manly Man looks at me for so long that I wonder what he must be thinking. Finally, he clears his throat and whispers.

"Your daughter is beautiful, very beautiful."

A smile creeps on Father's lips. "She is my carboncopy."

"Look at how fast she's growing. Very soon, she'll be married. I have a suitor in mind. He's a fair and handsome man. I know she'll like him," he laughs.

I want to throw my hands across his face, to give him a slap. I want to tell him he knows nothing about me, nothing about my preferences in men. But I smile and say nothing. Father pulls me to his side, kissing my forehead - a show of affection he would never display in private, a show of affection he saved only for public gatherings. He rubs my arm gently.

"She's fourteen?" Nnoja asks, referring to me.

Father nods vigorously and flashes his gapped teeth.

"Just ripe for marriage." Nnoja repeats. "Just ripe for marriage."

The men look at themselves for a while. They don't say a word, yet it's as though they are speaking with their eyes. I don't understand the communication going on between them, but suddenly Father releases me.

"Go. Go and dance with your sister."

"Next year, we might have another great cause to celebrate, a festival to hold if your daughter considers this suitor, which I speak of," Nnoja says softly.

I want to tell him that I do not plan to consider anybody's son, do not plan to get married… at least not now. Instead, I move to where Ugo and her friends are. They are taking turns shaking their bums in different rhythms under a tree.

When my eyes meet Ugo's, she pulls me close and asks if I am enjoying the festival. I shrug, and she smiles as though in pity, as though not understanding why anyone should not be happy in a time like this. I sit on a big stone and watch as Ugo whines her waist like a snake. The others praised her and took their turns. I wish I could whine my waist like that, and I decide that I will ask Ugo to teach me.

I drop my eyes to the ground and I stare at the small grains of sand, wondering how God could create something so small. After a few hours, I notice most people seem exhausted and tired, and children are slapping all over their bodies, accusing mosquitoes of not letting them sleep peacefully.

There is a full moon today - a sign that the gods are smiling on us. The Manly Men gulp palm wine until they are drunk, then they tell stories of how they got their heads. We don't go home until early in the morning.

When I get on my bed, I close my eyes and unbidden, I drift away into darkness. I see the head of Ada floating on the bank of the river. Her eyes are closed, and she seems to be sleeping peacefully. Suddenly, her eyelids twitch and her eyes shoot open. I am taken aback, scared of the piercing eyes looking deeply at me, at my soul.

"Come! Come! Let's celebrate the Festival of Heads!" she says.

I do not want to go. Yet, I find I have no control over myself. I find myself drawn to her, hypnotised by the fierce darkness in her eyes. I sigh, but I run towards the river, a burst of genuine laughter in my lungs. I spread my arms, saying, "Yes! Yes! Let's celebrate the Festival of Heads!"

Testimony Odey is a Nigerian teen writer, poet, and artist. When she is not reading or writing, you can find her watching Nollywood movies or scrolling through social media, where she encourages fellow Christians and makes new friends. Her first book, Uloma, won 2nd place in the Nigeria Prize for Teen Authors 2021 (Prose Category) and is currently being published.

A TRIP TO THE STARS

Adeboye Kanyinsola

It's Christmas eve again. It happens to be one of the days that deeply reminds me of my loss. I sat by the window as I watched the rainfall, the dew on the glass window as thewater drops raced down the panels. Tears rolled down my eyes as I tried not to think about what had happened in the past.

There is this popular adage that says that 'if you want to progress, don't live in the past', but that doesn't work here, not with me nor with my family. No matter how much we try, we remind ourselves of why we must be stuck in our past.

I wiped my tears as I stood up to go to my bed. Instead, my eyes went to the picture hung at the centre of the wall not too far from the door. There were other pictures and portraits.

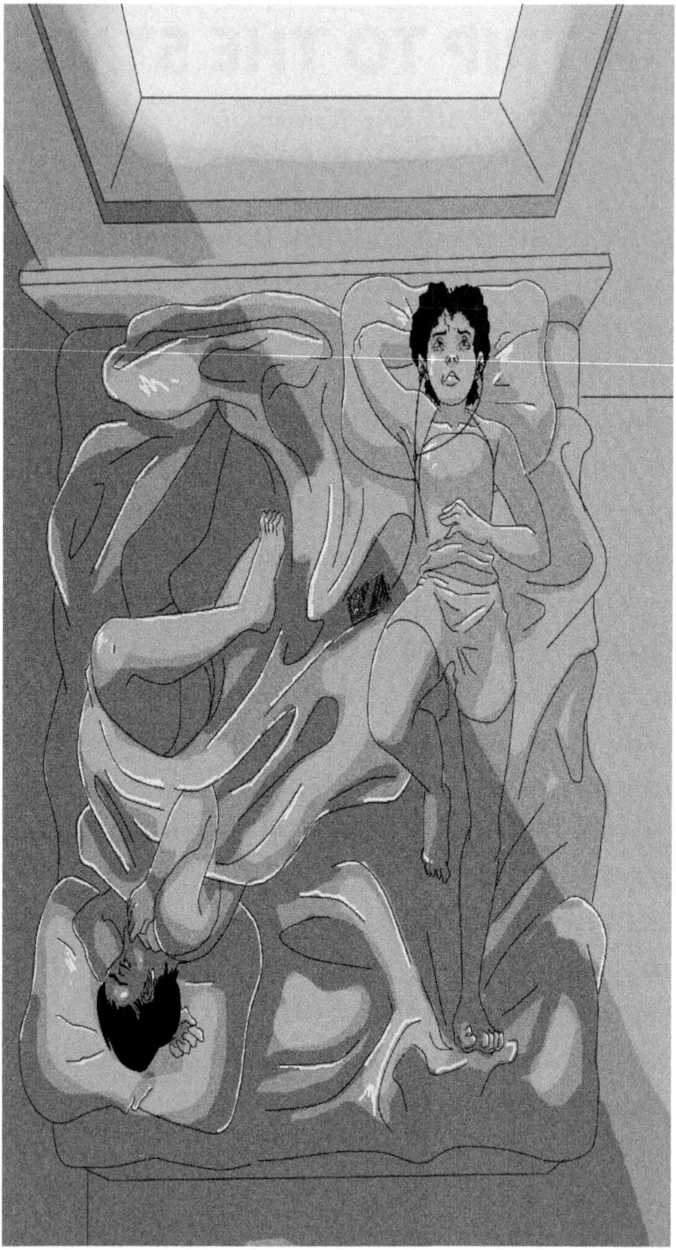

"Why does it have to be this one," I questioned my tears. I walked slowly towards the picture. I criedand held my breath. I felt the frame, the picture of my sister, my father and I. The last picture they took.

I looked up, holding onto the picture, and I could not possibly think of anything other than to end my life. I won't do that anyway. Even if I were to do that, I will tell you how it all started.

It was a bright day. Everything was fine. The best aroma was coming from my mother's kitchen. I ran into the kitchen smiling, being chased by my sister, Mary Ann. Mary Ann looks a lot like our mother, beautiful and tall, long hair, perfect eyebrows, chiselled face like a model. I had always, still do, idolize her my whole life.

"Bia ebe a," *If I catch you*. she said, laughing, running after me.

"Mommy, mommy, mommy," I shouted, not being able to breathe

because I was choked with laughter.

Mom smiled and called on to my sister. "Nkem," she continued, "Come help me with the dishes dear. Leave Chidi alone."

She squeezed her face at me and snapped her finger at me, and mouthed, 'I'll get you.'

Nkem and I set up the table as we awaited my brother and father. My brother worked for myfather. Since he was a child, he loved hanging out with our father, and they have more conversations than most married couples could ever have in their entire life.

Just after everything was already set, my father walked into the sitting room with my brother,Ben.

Ben, a very handsome man in his late twenties, broad shoulders and with teeth as white as snow, he strongly resembles our mother with both temperament and appearance.

My mother is meek, lovable, gentle, and kind. I wished I was like her most of the time. I am not gentle in any way, and

I cannot control my anger. I have anger issues, just like my father.

We settled down to eat. Mom happens to be the best cook in the world. We ate in silence andin twenty minutes, we were done. I cleared the dishes, and Emeka washed them. Emeka works in the house as a steward, and he has been doing that for years now.

I went up the stairs to my room to complete my assignments, and I heard an argument coming from my parents' room. Even when you think things are smooth, there is always aproblem.

Nkem and Ben were already rushing in the direction of their room. I just stared, being unableto do nothing, I was helpless.

"Leave this place!" I heard my mom screaming at my siblings, and crying. They peered at her, not knowing what to do. "Go away," she screamed louder. "Now!"

She slammed the door on their faces. I ran to Nkem who was already crying. "Whathappened?" I asked.

"Nothing," she sobbed. "Nothing

happened."

"You can't just tell me nothing happened. Nkem, talk to me. Please Nkem. Please," I begged. "Leave me alone... please," she whispered, giving me a message through her eyes.

We walked back to our rooms. I shared a room with Nkem because I was afraid of the darkness. She wasn't scared of anything: since the day I have known her, she has no fears, but today was different. I saw fear and other emotions too difficult to describe.

I wanted answers, what happened? Why did mom scream? Why was dad yelling? What did Ben and Nkem see when they got there? Why did my parents refuse help? Just too many questions without answers. I know Ben won't answer me and Nkem is not in her right state ofmind. I just hope Mom and Dad are fine, I hope so.

Nkem was sleeping beside me in a parallel way, folded on her side, backing me and facing the wall, as she used her blanket to cover herself.

"Nkem," I called. "Nkem, are you

asleep?"

No response. She wasn't going to answer even if she wasn't asleep. "Sleep tight, Sis." I switched off the light and slept on my back, staring at the ceiling. I took my earphones andplayed *Runaway* by *Aurora* and slept off.

Just like every other night after that day, it continued. I found out that Dad has been violent. He was always beating her because of little mistakes. Beat her for no reason too. It is just crazy how my father beats my mom.

Mom was no longer herself. She was not happy anymore. I could not stand my father. He smiled too much; you'd think he is the best man in the universe. Well, he used to be but not now.I hope my mom does something about it fast before it gets out of hand.

I walked home in silence as my friends,

and I walked past Allen Avenue in the evening. It was a cool evening, and the sun was starting to set.

Completing secondary school can be utterly difficult. The stress was enough and being in Art and Humanities means you have a lot to read.

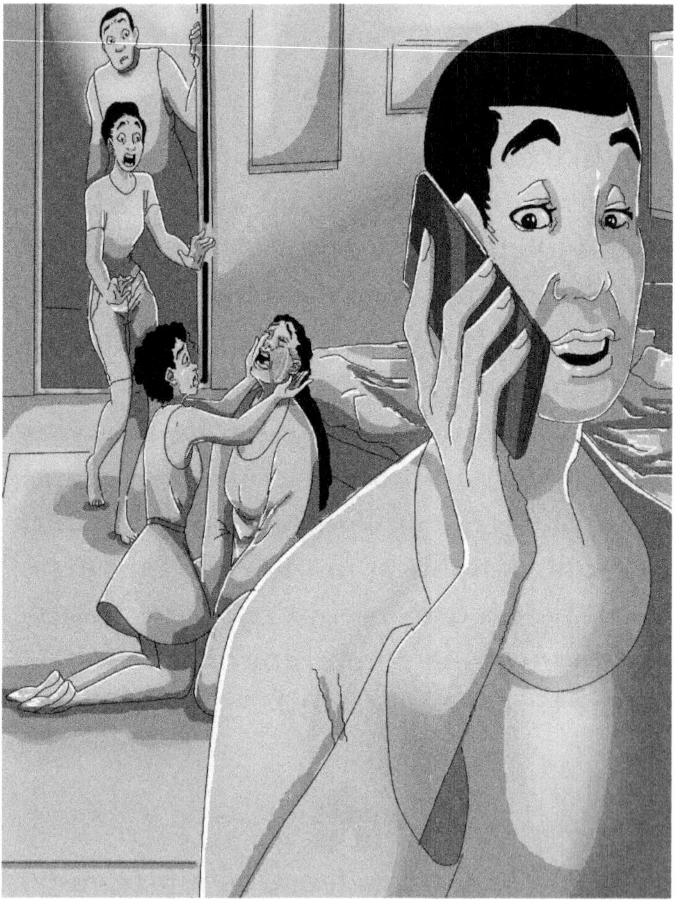

We get to close 6pm in the evening. I couldn't stop thinking about everything that had happened to me. I felt left out, although my friends weren't putting me out. We parted ways at Kukoyi Road.

"Hey. Bye," beamed Ikeme.

I took Keke Napep, which dropped me at the front of the Estate's gate. My house is just a few blocks away. I decided to get junks and a voucher for data at the mart just after the estategate.

I used the doorbell, and Emeka came just in time to open the door. His face lit up themoment he saw me.

"Small madam, welcome."

"Uncle Emeka, good evening." I smiled. "How you dey?"

"I'm fine, I'm fine."

"I dey go buy something for Madam, I dey come."

"Oh, Mom is back?"

"Ee."

I closed the gate behind him. Emeka has been our steward for a decade now, and he hasbeen trustworthy. He is also related to my late grandma.

As I walked into the house, I saw my mom's eyes fixated on the LED TV. "Hey, mom," I greeted

"How are you? Freshen up and come and eat. Your dad and siblings will be home in twentyminutes."

"OK. I hope you are fine too."

"Yes, I am," she smiled, not genuinely.

I walked up the stairs and went to my room, deep in my own thoughts. When dad comes back, I pray he will be a good man and not be aggressive anymore. I undressed, took my bath, and wore my play clothes.

I love writing poems, everyone knows, but sometimes, it seems difficult to think with everything that's wrong but, I decided to write. After writing and crosschecking it and correcting my mistakes, I wrote something:

A little lie will do when you become pretentious.

It now becomes a pleasure of anticipation.

For me, when you become silent,

Your silence is not silent,

why?
I get to speak.

A little lie will do while.
I get excited and prepared when you need answers.
Your answers can be suited for your questions.
yet not correct,
why?
I am your answer.

This pain, this grief you make me feel
does not add up to those little lies.
Tiny little lies to loved ones?
Little lies to cover the previous ones?
Yes, a little lie will do,
little lie eliminates and builds,
just a little lie.

I cleared my papers and pencil box and tidied up my room. Afterward I went downstairs and set up the table for everyone as we waited for my dad. I wasn't really expecting mybrother back today though, he now hardly comes home because he got himself an apartment.

They came and freshened up, and we all settled down for the meal. Dad prayed over the food, and we served ourselves. "How was the trip?" I asked.

"It was good, very good," Dad said. "We met Jacqueline, your French tutor, at the exhibit. She came with her fiancée."

"Yeah, it was beautiful," Nkem added.

"Ben?" I smiled, looking at him.

"The trip was good. What else do you want me to say?" He raised his left brow and chuckled, then winked and said, "Later, leave me. I want to eat." Unlike the rest of us, he could speak Yoruba fluently.

"How was today, dear?" Dad asked.

"Well, how was today, Chidi?" Mom asked.

They asked me almost at the same time.

"It was—" Dad's spoon interrupted me; he slammed his spoon against his plate, wiped his mouth, dropped it on his plate, and stood up to go upstairs.

"What was that? Mom! Answer me, what was that?"

"You saw for yourself."

It is Christmas Eve, for heaven's sake. He shouldn't be acting this way. I pray he does not beat her this night.

Early the next day, after what happened yesterday, I thought my father had changed a little bit,you know, sometimes annoyed but not beating her.

Christmas in the air. Deck the halls with boughs of holly. Hurray! The sun was bright, cool, and the birds were singing. You could feel the festivity in the air. Until I heard a loud cry.

My mom was wailing. I ran as fast as possible to her room. Nkem ran after me calling my name, but I did not answer. Mom was crying with too many bruises on her face. Dad was tellingus to keep quiet because he was on a call smiling.

I ran at him with all my might to push him and cause his phone to fall off. He swerved andcame at me.

Nkem shouted: "No!"

Dad took her instead and threw her so hard against the wall that she could not move, and she wasn't truly moving. I thought she fainted, but then, I moved close and felt her pulse.

Ben was here already. Today is Christmas day. We love spending time together as a family, and we do invite friends.

Ben came close and mom forgot everything that was happening to her and crawled to my side. Nkem was in my hands. I was shaking her, but she didn't move.

My brother lifted her from the ground and rushed her into the car. Father said he was going to follow them. Everyone wanted to go, but Ben told mom and I to stay back at home.

After they left, I helped my mom up and hugged her. She hugged me back, and then she pulled away, held my gaze, and wiped my tears away. My mother gave me words of affirmation that things would be better and that I should not worry about her. She wouldn't let me talk, though I did not know what to say at that moment anyway. I just kept on crying.

An hour later, we got a call. My mom

stood up to pick up her phone to receive the call. I just kept staring at her. She answered the call, and the person told her something. All I know is the phone fell, and she stood still, unable to move.

Well, let me just say my daddy, brother, and sister, dead, in the fatal accident. My mom's sanity died that day too. On Christmas day.

After that day, my mother didn't talk to me like she used to anymore. She feels like I caused thewhole thing. She could not bear it, and neither could I but that doesn't mean I caused it.

Nevertheless, I blame myself for our loss. It has been two years now. If only I had just stayedwith my mom. If I had not gone for dad, Nkem would not have died, Ben would not have been involved in that accident. If only...

Today, I still blame myself for what happened that day. As I took the rope I purchased from the supermart to hang myself crying heavily, I heard a knock on my door. I wished it wasn't my mom, but I know she is the one. I wiped my tears and hid the rope under the bed. I opened the door, and she came in. To be very honest, I wasn't expecting her. It has been a year since shelast came to me like this.

"Mom, what are you doi—"

"No, darling. I should be doing the talking," she blurted in right away.

"I should not have treated you like that for the past two years, baby. I know you've blamed yourself so much. I'm sorry. I've not been there when you needed me." A tear found its waydown from the corner of her eyes. "I'm sorry about your father and your siblings. Your father maltreated me, baby. I should have done something earlier."

"I beg of you, please don't let anyone maltreat you. Domestic violence is bad. It has killed morewomen in the world than most diseases."

"Mom, why? Why did he maltreat you though?"

"He... He was cheating on me and I found out about it, not intentionally but someone sent him a message and I went to give him his phone. He accused me of going through his phone and that I have seen what I was not supposed to have seen, and it started gradually, baby," she paused. "I really want a better life for you, but please always reach out for help. No matter how small the abuse might seem, physical, emotional or mental abuse always reach out for help."

She smiled and hugged me and said, "I love you, darling, never forget." She stood up.

"I love you too, mom."

"Bye. Sleep tight," she said and blew me a kiss.

I woke up the next day feeling good.

It was a bright day, and everything was fine. The best aroma was coming from my mother's kitchen. This is deja vu, only without my sister pursuing me around.

I went into the kitchen and hugged my mom. "Good morning, mom."

"Lovie, how are you?" she asked.

"I am fine, mommy."

Then she dived into a big gist. It has been a long time since I last saw my mom this happy. This means a lot to me. My mom being happy is festive enough, the stars around her are just too bright.

The stars are far away but not beyond our reach. The stars we want might be in utopia, but that doesn't mean we can't still reach them in reality.

These stars should be celebrated and embraced. Stars might not shine due to dust; when the dust is gone, the glory returns.

Journeying to the stars might look like a long trip, but we don't give up until we get to our destination. The stars are pulchritudinous: Don't give up until you get to them.

This is the best Christmas. My mom's happiness was the festive part for me, and we both reachedfor the stars. It was a wonderful trip.

"Oops, the pancakes got burnt but baby, do you mind telling me that funny story one moretime?" Mom asked with a grimace.

“Sure,” I answered, and we guffawed.

THE CHRISTMAS OF '98

Chekwube Ejiofor

Christmas season was the best time of the year for me. I looked forward to every Christmas holiday right after the last one. The festivities that come with the season thrilled and delighted me, it is the distinct smell of the harmattan that comes late September after the rains stop, then follows, the shopping, decorations, carols, and of course the array of delicious meals which you don't get to eat all year round but are only specially cooked during the season.

The best part is getting to buy new dresses and shoes to show off to your friends and enemies alike. I loved decorating the house with mum and she knew I loved doing it with her, so she always waited for me to vacate from the boarding school before putting up the decorations and the Christmas tree.

It usually would be a few weeks to Christmas

before I vacate school so once I get home, I would only have a few days rest before I and mum would hurry to the market to get me new dresses and shoes and also do her Christmas shopping. My Christmas hair would be left to a few days before Christmas so it would still remain neat and intact.

The days leading up to the 25th were extra exciting. I would help mum prep the ingredients for our Christmas food, bake cakes and fry some *chin-chin* and on Christmas morning, we would attend the early morning mass, then come back home and immediately start cooking our Christmas food, which always consisted mainly of fried and jollof rice, coleslaw, and chicken. Then mum would dish out some of the food to be distributed to the neighbours and whenever I went on those errands, I always came back bearing gifts, especially monetary gifts, which I saved for the outing on the twenty-seventh with my best friend Shalom where we would go out to the park or any fun place in town to enjoy ourselves and of course buy anything we wanted with the money we made on Christmas day. We would spend time together talking about everything and anything, and as we both went to different schools; we made the most of our outing since we weren't going to see again till the next holiday.

This was our ritual every year until the

Christmas of 1998.

It was the Christmas holiday again and everyone was in a festive mood. I had just vacated from school, coming out the top of my class with the first position boldly printed on my report sheet. I was excited because I knew I would have Mum and Dad at my fingertips, and I could ask them for anything I wanted, and they wouldn't say no to me. Mum was so proud she called all my aunties to tell them her *'Ada nwanyi'* came out first position. My dad tried to hide his happiness, which was a typical Nigerian parent, as if his expressing it would make me fail the next term, but nonetheless, I knew he was happy and proud of me.

Preparations began in top gear as usual. Mum and I went food and clothes shopping, decorated the house and the Christmas tree together and simple meals while we prepped ingredients for the main cooking, which would happen on Christmas morning. Christmas day came and went, and then came the 27th when I and Shalom would go for our outing.

I woke up that morning with a stomach-ache, but I attributed it to all the food I had eaten on Christmas day. Dad had travelled the week before for a meeting in the village that took place every December, so it was just me and mum at home. Mum told me to cancel with Shalom since I wasn't feeling well, and dad wasn't around to drop me off, but I insisted on going because I knew I wouldn't be able to see her again till the next holiday. Mum dropped me off at our usual rendezvous, which was the park. We had so much fun together that day that we both didn't want to go back home.

Usually, Shalom's dad comes to pick us up, but he had fallen ill so he made sure to give Shalom some money for a taxi that'll take us both home. We felt like big girls taking a taxi home with no adult in our company. We flagged down the first taxi that honked past and entered, making sure to instruct him on our different drop-off points. We both sat in the backseat, having our last-minute gist before we departed. Neither of us noticed when the driver veered off our route; neither did we notice when he sprayed something that made us pass out.

Whenever the 'ember months, which begin in September to December approach everyone was to apply extra caution as those were the months where ritual killings by occult men take place, and the rate of crime increases as everyone is trying to meetup to their Christmas obligations either by hook or by crook. Those were myths or so I thought I always heard while growing up, but I had never put my mind to it I only watched it on home videos. Now, it was happening to me live and I couldn't believe my eyes.

I and Shalom woke up tied to a tree in the middle of a makeshift camp set up deep inside the bush of God knew where. There were others there, mostly kids and teenagers I guessed were between the ages of 2-16 years. They hardly gave us food or water, and in my presence, two little kids died. Every evening two men clad in all black and a hood would come to pick up at least two children.

I asked one of the girls that looked my age where they usually take the children. She said to the slaughter room. Cold shivers ran down my spine. The home videos I and mum watched was playing out right before me. I couldn't understand how humans became this wicked and heartless. Shalom never stopped crying. I would say I was the strongest between us, constantly trying my best to calm her fears as much as I could, even though deep down, the same fear was crippling me. I told her we had to be strong and never stop praying to God because he was our sure hope of getting out alive.

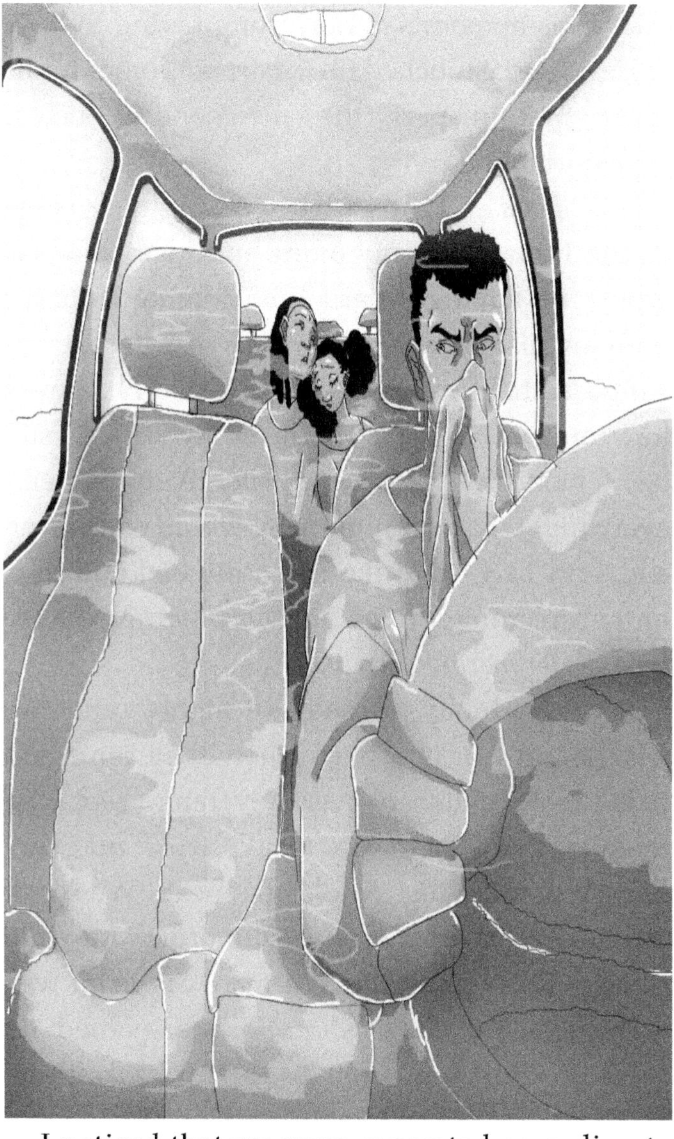

I noticed that we were separated according to

our age, and one morning, I overheard one of the guards as he points at our group saying that we were not to be touched till Chairman comes for he must first inspect the merchandise before transportation.

Merchandise! That's what we were now being called. I thought of my mum, and I was sure she would be having a hard time coming to terms with my disappearance during a season that was supposed to be merry and joyous, and I had even lost count of the days that went by with us still being held captive. I prayed silently in my heart every night that this nightmare would come to an end, and I would wake up in my bed and hear mum screaming my name: "*Onyinyechi wake up! It's time for morning devotion*."

Day gradually turned to nights, and we watched in fear and horror how they came and took away children every evening, replacing them by noon the next day. We woke up every day, not knowing who'd be next. We were awoken one early morning with orders for us to stand in line, finally, the chairman was on his way to inspect the *merchandise.* So, we queued up according to our groups. I kept reassuring Shalom that God will not let anything happen to

us. We were about twenty in our group of only teenage girls.

Chairman finally arrived later that afternoon; he was a middle-aged man with average height and looked just like any regular man on the street. I noticed he wore a wedding band which must mean he had a family and most probably kids, just like all of us currently being kidnapped and held against our will; we all had parents, family and friends that were worried about our whereabouts. He approached each girl sizing them up and down, back and front. A nod meant you were good 'merchandise', but a hand wave meant you needed to be sent away.

I prayed that I and Shalom would get a hand wave, but I felt sorry for the girls that got a nod. I could only but imagine their lot. When he came up to me, I felt my heart in my mouth. All I remember saying in my mind was: *please God, give me a hand wave.* He raised my chin, turned it from side to side, gave me a once over, and waved his hand doing same for Shalom.

It had already been two weeks into the year of 1999, the day my mum, my dad and Shalom's mum and dad picked us up after they'd blindfolded us, threw us out of a moving vehicle in Zaria and no were close to Abuja where we lived.

Seeing my parents felt like I was being given a second chance at life, and I prayed not my experience on anybody, not even an enemy. Integrating back into society was difficult especially going out alone. I either went with my dad or mum, and any strange look or glance from anyone meant tagging them a kidnapper, and of course, entering taxis were completely crossed out of my list.

The festive season was no longer festive for me. Whenever the Christmas holidays approached, I began to have panic attacks, and it just brought back sad and scary memories, but with time, I slowly began to bury it, pushing it back into my subconscious till it became an unforgettable distant memory.

Chekwube Ejiofor is an Accountant with a passion for writing. Writing transports her to a world where there are no boundaries, and her imagination is free to run wild, which indeed is really beautiful. When she's not writing, she enjoys watching *Telemundo* series, reading and eating.

ENI ITAN

Babs Iwalewa

Enitan woke up suddenly in the middle of the night, perspiring heavily; the white bedspread was heavily patched and wet from the excessive sweat coming out of his body. The water coming out of his body was not normal as he had slept in his boxer shorts and singlet, and the *OX* electrical fan and the split AC in his room were working at maximum capacity.

It was not his fault that he couldn't sleep; these cycles of insomnia had become a regular feature of his life in the last three weeks or so, particularly since the gale of job cuts and retrenchment started at Dodonkodi Bank where he works. Within the last three weeks, Enitan had watched helplessly as the gale of retrenchment swept away his manager, and even close confidants at work. At the last count, over twenty-five members of staff had been laid off at the branch where he worked in what the management said was the first batch of the retrenchment exercise.

Enitan got up from the bed dripping with sweat as if he had just taken a shower. He pulled off his singlet and went into the living room, where he proceeded to switch on the light. What he saw further depressed him; his living room was tastefully furnished with a 32-inch plasma TV firmly glued to the wall complemented by the large home theatre multipurpose audio-visual musical set with giant speakers. The dining section of the living room had imported glass dining chairs and tables. The whole living room was rugged with Arabian carpets while two split air conditioning systems adequately ventilated the living room.

Enitan shivered and wondered how he was going to be able to maintain his present lifestyle, supposing the inevitable happened. He sat down on one of the sofas, and he put on the TV. He checked the wall clock, and he discovered it was just past midnight. He attempted to change the channels on the TV in an effort to steady his nerves by watching TV. He soon discovered he wasn't making any headway; he threw away the remote control and sank his whole frame into the sofa with his face buried in his two palms.

His mind raced fast to the past. He remembered how he had struggled through

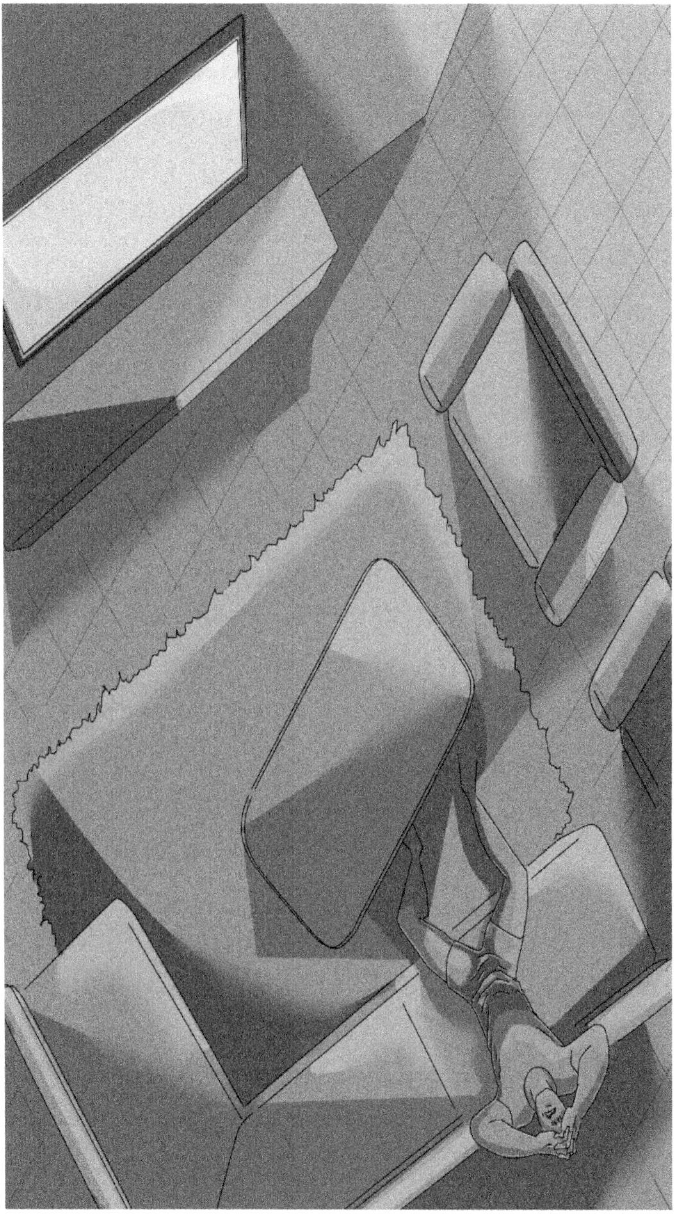

school, having lost his parents when he was still a child - he had been raised by a distant aunt, who also struggled through life that most of the time, she found it almost impossible to provide him with essentials, talk less of anything extra while he was growing up.

He had gone through the University by his own sheer will and determination. He suffered indignities and deprivations, but he persisted. And his efforts were crowned when he graduated and secured a job immediately with *Dodonkodi Bank* as an Executive Trainee. This period marked a turning point in his life, as his emoluments which were in the realm of a six-digit figure per annum, completely transformed him.

It had been two years now that he had been in the employ of *Dodonkodi Bank,* and Enitan had transformed into a swashbuckling, haughty, and rich twenty-six-year-old young man. He completely embraced the good life, he drove one of the best automobiles in town; he had rented a two-bedroom apartment in the upscale section of town, he travelled first class, he drank exotic wines, he ate outlandish cuisines and courted the most beautiful girls in town, and he seemingly enjoyed the good life while it lasted. But before one could whisper 'economic recession', the good life he enjoyed became threatened with the "gale" and "tsunamis" of job cuts in his bank. Enitan's case had been made worse by the fact that he had contacted a soothsayer at the onset of the retrenchments, and he had been told in no uncertain terms that he would surely be sacked before the end of the retrenchment exercises in his bank.

Where do I start from? He muttered out from his recumbent position on the sofa.

"Aaah! *Igboro ti daru!*" he exclaimed nervously as he remembered that although so much money and opportunities had passed through his hands in the last two years, he had not achieved any transcendental transformation in his personal life, talk less of in the lives of people who were close to him

Suddenly, his old aunt's constant chorus of '*ranti omo eniti iwon se*', which were admonitions to him to remember his humble roots but which he unfortunately never took heed of began to make sense to him. He jerked as the alarm clock from his bedroom began to make its presence felt subtly across the whole apartment.

He had not slept at all, and he needed to start getting ready for work as he looked at the wall clock in the living room and discovered it was

6am. He shrugged and shivered as he remembered that the last batch of retrenchment exercise in his office was slated for today. As he made straight for the bathroom, he brushed his teeth and stepped into the shower. With cold water splattering all over his body while he stood under the shower motionless and lost in thought.

Pon! Pon!! Pon!!!

His neighbour's car horn jolted him out of his reverie as he realized that his neighbour was already set for work and was waiting for him to come and pull his car that was parked at the rear of his neighbour's car out of the way. He dashed out of the bathroom naked with water dripping all over his body, straight into his bedroom, where he quickly got dressed for work with his neighbour still pressing his car horn as if he was rehearsing for a musical concert. He got out of his apartment, apologising profusely to his neighbour, who ignored him with so much disdain written on his face.

On getting to work, he went straight to his desk. Surprisingly he discovered he could not gain access to the computer on his desk. He shivered, and a creeping cold sensation knocked his spine.

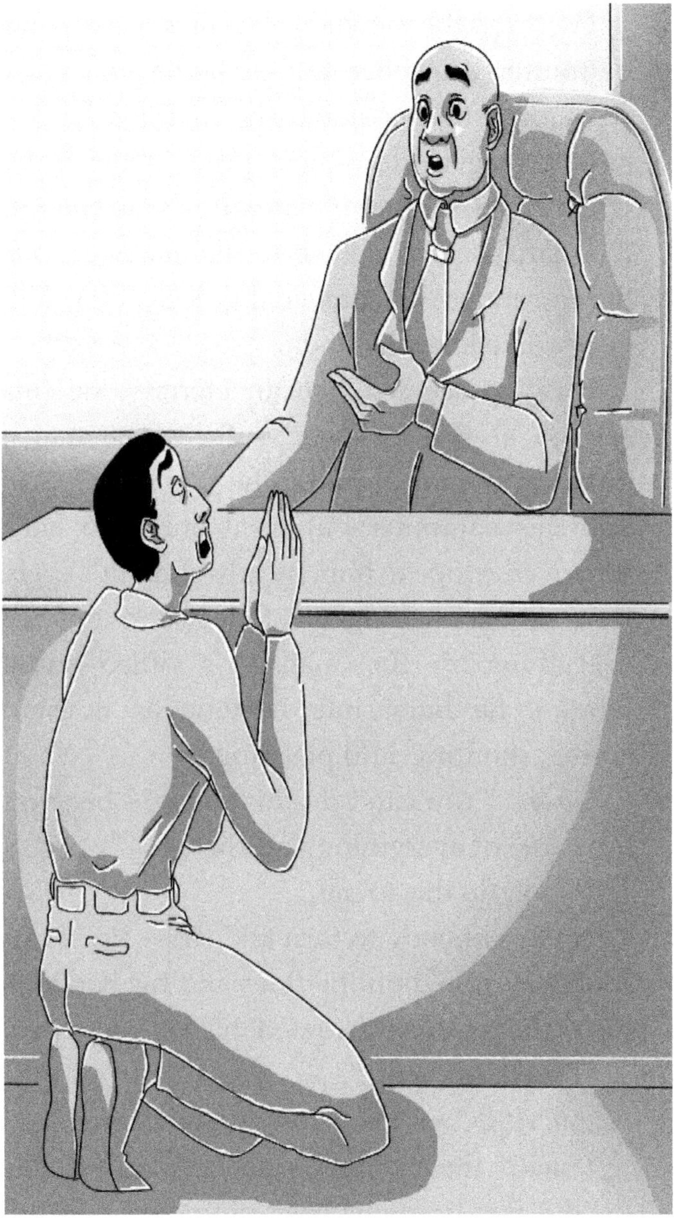

"Perhaps the inevitable has finally happened," he muttered incoherently as he began to sweat. And almost immediately, he was sent for by the new manager. He almost peed in his trousers when he heard that his attention was sought by the manager. He walked to the manager's office dazed, and as he moved his legs, they felt so heavy, like logs of wood.

In what seemed like an eternity, he finally arrived at the manager's office. The manager didn't even look at him as he was busy working with his computer but went ahead to hand a brown envelope to him. By now, Enitan's eyeballs were almost popping out of their sockets as he felt everything in the manager's office swirling around; he burst into hysteria as he started crying, shouting, and pleading…

No sir! "You can't do this to me. I beg you in the name of everything you cherish."

"Don't do this to me."

"I have nobody to turn to!" *Please sir…!* As he spoke, he rolled on the floor and his hands held the manager's feet. Irritated, his boss snapped:

"Do what to you?"

Ah! Ah!! "Sir, I beg you don't sack me."

"Sack?" the manager squeaked, astonished.

"But you have just been promoted, and this is

your letter." He waved the letter which Enitan had refused to collect.

"P-r-o-m-o-t-i-o-n?" Enitan asked like a drunk.

"Yes," the manager reaffirmed

On hearing this, Enitan passed out.

Babs Iwalewa is a self-motivated writer and has contributed articles to several local, international, and online dailies/journals. He has several unpublished short stories and poems that had taken a back seat until now. He was the secretary (Caretaker Committee) of the Association of Nigerian Authors Kaduna State chapter from 2010 to 2011.

THE BOND THAT BINDS YOU

Joseph Jegede

It was the last day in August, the day you last had an argument with your mother, the day she last slapped you for your unseriousness, the day she last pulled you by the ear and scolded you for spending too much time writing lyrics of songs when you should be solving math, the day you raised your voice at her for the first time for demanding too much from you, the day you told her you were an adult and knew what was good for you even at sixteen, the day you told her to stop embarrassing you, the day she slapped you on the cheeks for raising your voice at her, and you saw series of stars. The day that your father arrived and intervened.

It was not the day when she walked into your room very early in the morning holding a motivational book titled MAKE HAY WHILE THE SUN SHINES and exhorted you from it on how you should be more serious with your academics. Not the day when she told you she was disappointed in you for failing WAEC, and you had explained that you only failed mathematics without which you could even proceed to the university as an art student.

It was not the day either when she found out you already had a boyfriend. Well, that was a long time ago. She had suspected you when you told her you felt like taking a stroll down the estate. She had consented but secretly instructed Isila, the housemaid, to trail you and give her a report. Isila had brought the report of you meeting a boy under the mango tree towards the entrance of the estate.

Isila had told her how you laughed at the jokes your lover cracked, she had told her how she couldn't keep her eyes open when she realized that the two of you were going to kiss each other, she had told her how you let the boy spank your buttocks, and you told him you liked it. You liked the way he grabbed your ass.

Isila had further told her of how your boyfriend kept asking when you would come over to his place, and you kept giving excuses making him understand that your mummy said you would get pregnant.

"My mummy said if I do it, I would get pregnant. She said if a man touches me, I would get pregnant, and I don't want to be pregnant yet," you had said, and he had convinced you that your mother was not enlightened enough.

Isila further told her how she ran back home when she realized that you had caught her spying on you. You had returned home that day in fear hoping to be scolded as usual by your mother, but nothing of such happened. Not on that day.

And it was not on the next day either when your mother had unusually knocked before entering your room and when she finally entered, she sat you down and made you see reasons why you should not think of a man at this moment. She had pointed out the fact that it could ruin whatever career you are pursuing, even your music. And it hadn't occurred to you that she had brought music into the conversation because she knew that was the only thing you cared about.

Nonetheless, the words sunk into your brain that day. Later in the evening, when Chuks, your boyfriend, called, you told him you were no longer interested and hung up even before he protested why. He kept calling your phone, and you refused to pick up.

And when you realized he wouldn't stop calling, you sent him a text reaffirming your stance and blocked his line so that he wouldn't be

able to reach you again. That was the first time you took your mother's words seriously. But it was not the day which you would forever remember.

It was rather the day you swore never to forgive yourself for. It was the day you went out with your father. You let yourself reminisce on how it all started that day. Your mother had caught you writing songs after she had instructed you to go solve some math equation. You got to your room and did otherwise. You didn't see any reason why you should rewrite WAEC, like she was insisting.

She wanted you to rewrite your SSCE (Senior School Certificate Examination) because you didn't pass mathematics in the previous one. You busy yourself instead with some music in your room. You sat down at the little table in your room, which you shared with no one. The bedspread was rumpled. It was evident you had spent quite some time in that bed before you settled in the plastic chair at the table.

You looked at yourself in the mirror and let your hands journey around your lips. You liked how round they were; you admired yourself for a moment before finally picking up your pen to write your lyrics. You lift your head up at intervals like the lyrics were falling from the sky or as if what you wanted to write was glued to the ceiling.

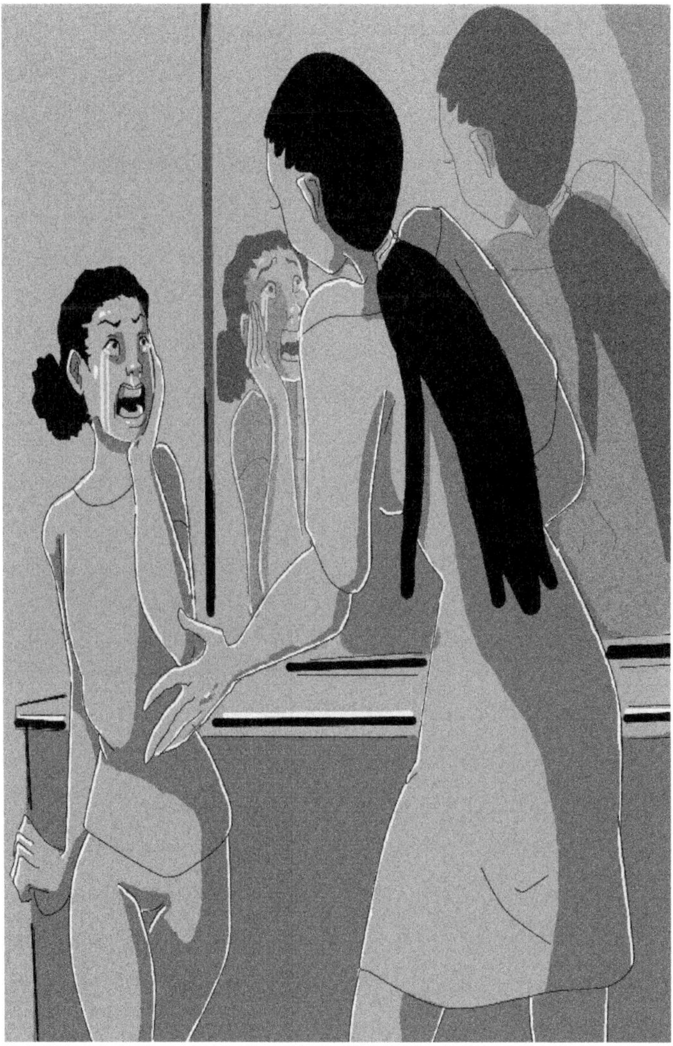

Sometimes, you took your eyes off the ceiling to the air conditioner, which was lying somewhere in the corner of the room in its rectangle form, opening and closing to make the room cold. You kept writing, and a bead of sweat dropped on your sheet. You looked up at the air conditioner and wondered if it wasn't cold enough. But you knew it was cold; the rest of your body felt cold, except for your head, which was hot. You guessed it could have been because you were racking your brain so hard for the lyrics to rhyme.

Nonetheless, you picked up the remote control of the air conditioner and controlled it from nineteen to sixteen, hoping this time that it would be cooler. It did work as the sweat started to dry up gradually until the door to your room flung open, and your mother barged in.

She looked furious as she asked you why you were so stubborn. You told her you were about to start your mathematics, but she said you lied. She slapped you. You didn't know whether the slap was because you lied or because of your stubbornness. You didn't have time to know as your eyes saw stars in small glistening shades. Your vision was transiently tampered with; you staggered but soon regained your stance.

Now you are furious with her for slapping you. You didn't know where you got the courage from. Even now, you still wonder what had come over you then, but it doesn't matter again. You screamed and shouted at her for refusing to believe in you; in your dream, you shouted at her for slapping you. Although she wouldn't have guessed, you also shouted at her for all the hate you've nursed against her. And yes, it was that day that things changed. You never knew that day that things would forever change, but they did. It was that day that your daddy died.

After the encounter with your mother, you had grown moody. Your father soon returned from work, and your mother narrated her own part of the tale to him in their bedroom. You were sure she would have exaggerated everything, but there was no room for you to counter.

Your daddy soon came to you and asked you what happened. You found yourself crying as you started to talk. He was moved and emotional. He hated to see you cry. He hated to see his baby cry. He volunteered to take you out so you could cheer up. You both got into his black Toyota Camry. And he drove you around Ibadan while you sang some of your songs to him, doing various riffs and runs in between and even pitching unnecessarily, not minding the noise that could cause. You both enjoyed the moment as you laughed uncontrollably.

For a while, you forgot your worries and your mood got lighter. You felt suddenly moved to give your daddy a hug after ruminating on how caring and supportive he had been in your life, not minding that he was driving. It was the last you gave to him and the last he received from you. He lost control of the steering, and the car tumbled into a ditch just after the Asejire bridge. You screamed Jesus! But that was the last thing you said until help came.

Moments later, you were lifted up into a stretcher. The car had got locked during the accident. The helpers had to break through the windows of the car to drag both you and your daddy out just before the Road Rescue Team arrived at the scene. You were not brutally injured. You only bruised your forehead, but they insisted you got to the hospital for further examination. You didn't get the chance to see your father. They didn't let you see him as you were separately attended to. And when you asked of him, they said he was fine, that he was receiving treatment.

It soon got broken to you that your father had

passed away. You couldn't ask if it was due to shock or he had suffered some brutal injury. You were too pained to ask of anything. The thought of your mother soon came to you. What would she do? How would she feel? But she had heard of his death before you. You breathed successively as if your lungs were blocked, then you screamed. No one held you because the doctor said they should leave you to let out the grief. You were pained. You hated yourself. You hated the break of the day.

And now, as you stand elegantly in your blue jumpsuit and black high heels, with your face heavily painted of makeovers, you feel sober. It has been five years, and if not for you, your father would still have been alive. You blame yourself every day for it, even though your mother convinces you that you are not at fault.

Your guilt leads always to grief, like you are doing. Your mother tells you to cheer up, you've just signed a multimillion-naira deal with Freenation Music, but your P. Man, as you always referred to him, isn't here to witness this success. You wish he who never discouraged you from writing songs is alive to witness this day

You miss him. As you drive home away from Freenation's premises through the Asejire bridge, you feel a sharp hole in your chest, which only you can describe. This place brings back memories; it really does.

You drive a few meters from the bridge and park your car. You put off your shoes and step out barefoot. You elegantly walk down the steep river like a mermaid and sit on a stone. - P. Man, I miss you. You say as you throw a stone into the water. You don't know whether he can hear you wherever he is or not, but you are sure of one thing. The bond. You know that this place binds you.

During your father's funeral, you shed no tears, unlike the rest of the congregation, who shed torrential tears. You knew many of these people were just being hypocritical; some never knew him well, while some never knew him at all. You were the only one who knew him well, and he was the only one who knew you well. He was your best friend; you felt comfortable around him, but the days of your comforts were over, you thought.

You would never be able to run to anyone again after having a duel with your mother, nor sing your lyrics to anyone again. You knew things were never going to be the same again, especially as the undertakers, who, like every other member of the congregation, were dressed in black, lifted up the coffin in which your daddy was lying just a few seconds before the rain started. He's in a good place- Someone whispered to you, but you didn't even have the strength to look at whoever it was, you were, however, sure you heard a feminine voice. The rain started and beat the congregation, but no one left the rain. You all stood there at the Saint Thomas Cemetery, where the grave had been dug already.

You watched as they lifted the coffin into the empty hole and covered it. You watched as your mother wept bitterly with her hands stretched out towards the grave as if she could call out the dead. Her friends restrained her. Just before the grave was covered, you bent down, took sand in your hand and poured it on the coffin. You sprinkled it around it like salt just before the others started to take turns giving dust to dust. You watched the grave diggers covering the grave, and you heard as the first portion of sand escaped from the shovel onto the roof of the coffin in the grave. It made a loud sound, the kind of sound you usually heard whenever your mother was angrily banging your door.

You fell down to your knees, knowing that despite that disturbing sound, your father would never arise again. You wanted to cry, you longed for it, but the tears were not coming. Your mother walked up to you and knelt beside you in that rain. She wiped your face of imaginary tears and helped you up. You supported each other till you reached home.

Isila didn't bother to prepare solid food because she knew it would all waste, she only prepared hot tea and bread. She asked whether you would love to eat, but you didn't answer, neither did your mother. You walked upstairs instead and fell into your bed, not minding your soiled dress against the clean sheets of the bed. Memories of you and your P. Man on that Asejire bridge came back flooding to you, and you screamed.

You didn’t know for how long. Isila and your mother ran into your room to console you. Now, the tears which you had earlier searched frantically for started to rush down your face like the floodgates of heaven. You made no effort to resist as they came. You let the tears wet your face. You let grief take over you.

For days, you did not speak to anyone because you still could not get over the whole event on time. Your mother seemed to have quickly moved on. She had stopped grieving the next day, or so it seemed. When you saw her the next morning, she already looked different. Her head had been scraped to the bare. Widowhood duties, you knew.

Now, there was no way she would hide the shape of her oblong head under any braids or wigs. But that was the least of your concerns. You looked up to the pictures hung on the wall and saw one where you were sitting on your father's shoulders. He always said that was his favourite picture of life because he had you sitting on his shoulders while he kissed your mother. That way, you appeared taller than everyone in the picture. - that picture tells me you would be great in life, he always said. You couldn't stop your tears as you now looked at that picture. You walked back upstairs and locked yourself in your room.

You looked for your headphones but couldn't find them. You would do this without the headphones, you told yourself as you closed your eyes and started humming out tunes and writing them down. Hoping that one day, you will be able to dedicate them to him.

A fisherman is sailing on the Asejire River, and you look and admire the way he sails with his child, not minding that she is a girl. It reminds you of your father. But you don't want to think about the past again. While you sit there on the stone, you observe the torrents that fall from the dam afar and also the little stones that surround your seat, and you can't but remember your father again: of how he would let you play with stones as a kid, despite your mother's objection that you could soil your dress or get injured. 'Let her' - he would say and laugh it off. And again, for the umpteenth time, you can't stop thinking about him. You wish he hadn't died.

But perhaps it did you good that he died. It seemed like his death brought the reconciliation between you and your mother, you guess. Or does she blame herself too, like you do, for the death of your father? You sometimes think that if she had let you be on that fateful day, your P. Man might still be alive by now. Yet you know it would be wrong to ever make reference to that or make her feel this way.

Perhaps she realized it already because, since the funeral, she let you do whatever pleased you and did not scold you whenever you wrote songs. She only scolded you on other things which were not related to music. You began to admire her. And when one day she visited your room and asked you how the accident had happened, you had explained everything in detail but left out the part where you hugged him because you feared she might hate you for causing the death of her husband. How naive you were.

Your phone rings and you know it is your mother. She is worried you've not arrived home since you called you were on your way home. And when you told her you stopped by at Asejire, her tone changed. You know we should be celebrating- she says. But you know this is not a complete celebration. The one who gave the motivation is absent. You drop the phone and see the date on your home screen.

Second of September. It is exactly five years today. It's his death anniversary. If the dead really sees the living like they say, then you are sure he sees you from wherever he is. He sees his girl and must be really proud of the woman she's become, you think.

You stand up from the stone and begin to climb the steep up until you reach a levelled ground on the main road where your car is parked. You look down towards the river for the fisherman and his daughter, but they are out of sight. You open the door to your car and sit in it. You place your hand on the wheel. You know there is something you have to do before reaching home. Saint Thomas Cemetery. You would get flowers on your way.

You reach the cemetery and place the flowers gently on the grave of your father. You kneel at his feet and weep, resting your head on the grave. You search for words to say if he would hear, but none is even coming, and finally, the words come out, definitely not what you want to say, but what you ought to say. The utterance is a reflex as you open your mouth to say - thank you for all you did. And even in death, you believe he still watches over you.

Joseph Jegede is from Ondo state in Nigeria and is currently pursuing a degree at the Obafemi Awolowo University (OAU), Ile-Ife, Nigeria. In July 2021, he attended the Ludwig Maximillian University of München after he was awarded a summer school scholarship by the DAAD. He is a polyglot and a writer. He loves to read, write, and listen to music.

BONUS stories

PICTURESQUE

Agnes Kay-E

Ôffiôñg barely sank into the little chair in the pantry before her aunt's voice caused her to jump and straighten. She was exhausted, like a hair of the corn under the swelting sun. They had been cleaning the massive house for close to three days.

"Why are you there?" Ruth, Ôffiôñg's aunt, queried. "Go and clean the patio. I'm going out to get their foodstuff. Be done before I get back so we can leave."

"Yes, auntie," Ôffiôñg retorted and curtsied. Sighing ruefully, she trudged to the back of the house. Luckily, there was no grease, so cleaning and tidying was easy. The number of paintbrushes with clean bristles and old handles piqued her interest; they were held together by a string at the edge of a canvas lodged between two deck chairs. She pulled out the canvas and found it was a painting.

Disapproving how it was kept, she wrinkled her face, dusted it, and hung it up above what looked like a mantlepiece. Being the last of her

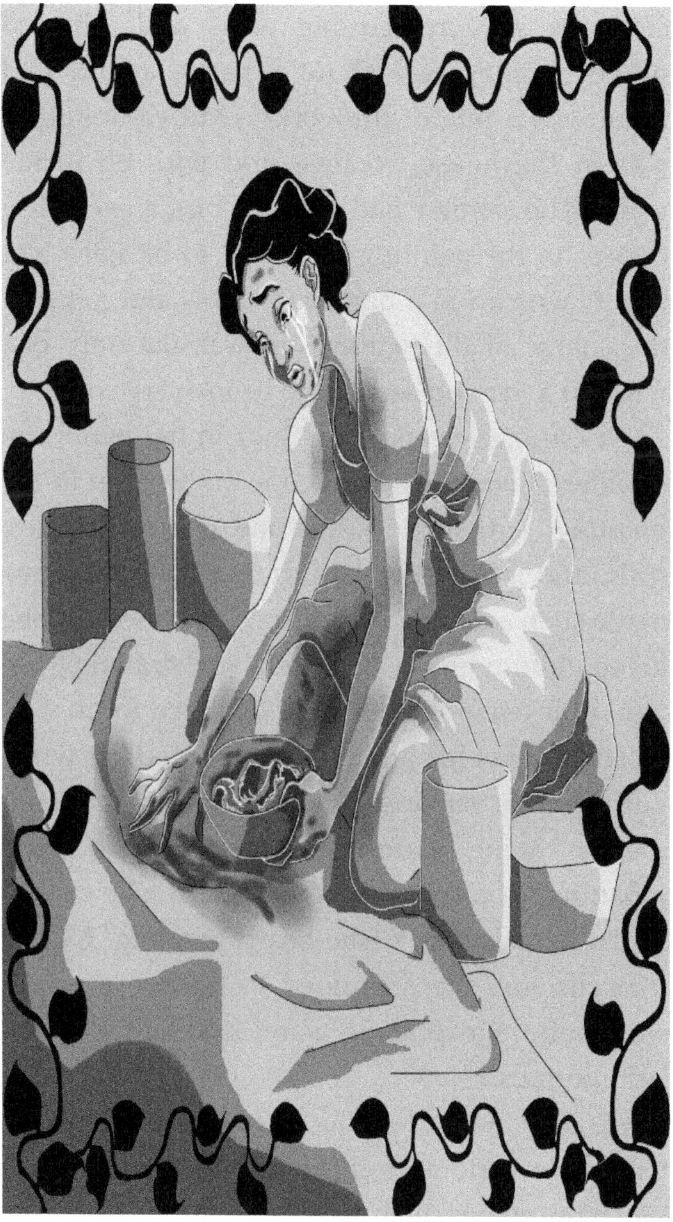

cleaning, she crossed her arms and admired it.The painting was about a party, at one end there was a pile of fireworks. Oddly enough, it was of the house, roofless and with no inside walls. The painter had taken a bird's eyes. The figures in the painting appeared to be staring at her. A woman in a dark blue dress and her hair the colour of the setting sun was the only one without a hat and seemed to be in every room.

As Ôffiôñg cleaned the door in the patio, she wondered what it was like for the women in the painting, with their satins and chiffon dresses, frills, and laces. They had to be wealthy to have made such a detailed painting of themselves. She loved chiffon and was particularly drawn to the light blue dress she'd seen and longed for it.

Thinking of her aunt, Ôffiôñg turned her wrist, guffawed in surprise, then hurriedly gathered their cleaning wares. Her bladder had been moaning for a while, so she went to take care of it. On her way back, she heard giggling. Not all that curious, she continued to the room where she'd left their cleaning wares and halted to the soft footfalls.

Ôffiôñg glanced at the wrist again. Her aunt would be furious if she was still in the house when the owners arrived. She saw someone in the softest blue dress run across the lawn and hid behind the door. Although she was curious about the new owners, she wasn't ready for her aunt's acerbic anger.

She waited until she was sure the owners weren't nearby; she hurried to the patio to gather her things. Sighing, Ôffiôñg returns to the patio to gather the rest of her things and couldn't help taking a cursory glance at the painting.

"I wish I had just an ounce of what they did," Ôffiôñg mumbled, sighed, and pursed her lips.

She frowned; something about it had been different. She moved closer. She was right. The woman in blue was fading, and everyone else seemed to be shying away from the sun – their lacy umbrellas were over their heads, concealing it. Beginning to suspect that hunger was taking its toll on her imagination, she sank onto the lone table.

In that instant, a light flashed, and Ôffiôñg glanced up at the painting. Suspecting it was the sun's reflection on something, she turned her gaze back to herself and bemoaned her uncultured nails, unruly hair and the acne on her face.

"I wish I could have their flawless skin. Oh, how I wish I were like those girls in the picture."

Ôffiôñg wrinkled her face at the sound of tearing and checked her dress. Relieved, she waved away at the buzzing sound, but there was no insect in sight. She exhaled heavily and straightened. The painting swayed and was about to fall, so she stretched her hands to catch it. She caught it wrong. Instead of her hands going through the tear in the painting, they went into it, and the colours from the painting threaded into the veins in her hands.

Frightened, she cried, "Aunty!"

Ôffiôñg could feel herself falling, her loud screaming echoed around her, but it was too dark to see. Suddenly she was on the floor. A little light, like the onset of sunrise, streamed in above her. She waited for her eyes to adjust to the dimness of the room and got up. Something caused the floor she was on to shudder. Thinking it was an earthquake, she lowered herself to the floor and covered her head.

A zipping sound followed, and the little light began to diminish. Ôffiôñg realised it was coming from the tear she'd made even though it didn't make sense as she hadn't actually torn the canvas.

She suspected it was her way in and therefore going to be her way out. She just needed to reach it. She jumped a couple of times but failed to reach the tear. In searching for something to use to reach it, she realised she couldn't move beyond the circumference of her arms' length.

She leaned against what seemed to be a barrier and ran a hand over it. It was ridged like the ones left by a rake except bigger.

"Where is your father?" a voice boomed around her.

Oh no! Aunty will kill me. I should have left the house o!

Ôffiôñg winced at a flickering sound; the light streaming in became stronger and jagged. It was still pitch black around her. She also noticed that when she looked down at the ridges and found she could see the room she was last in. She'd been told that the owner of the house's wife looked like Rita Dominic and wore blonde hair, and her stepdaughter looked like a short Kate Henshaw and bald.

"I don't know," the bald, Kate Henshaw lookalike answered and leaned over something Ôffiôñg suspected was the basket full of guava.

That is supposed to be mine. I didn't pick it for them o!

"Dee –"

"Only my friends are allowed to call me that. And you Roni are not," Dee snapped, glaring at Roni, Rita Dominic's lookalike.

"Did you give your snarky friend to your father to spite me?" Roni asked.

Dee clucked her tongue and opened the fridge.

"I knew it. You never liked me. You…" Roni bent over her buzzing phone and pressed it to her ear, and cried. "Where are your people? And I asked you to get rid of the painting, but you hung them back instead. I don't care about their beauty. As far as I'm concerned, they're grotesque. Fine. If you like them so much, you can come and get them. I want them out of this house now." Roni exhaled heavily and tapped her forehead. "On second thought, do it after the party."

Ôffiôñ gasped as the woman dropped her phone into the opening of a red, green and blue colour-block bag. She couldn't remain in one place, staring at the activities below her forever. She had to do something. Pondering, she tapped her toes.

Suppose there was a way to increase the tear.

Ôffiôñ shook her head.

The woman could see it and get rid of it before the party, and she'd be stuck in a closet forever.

"If I had known, I would have left it as it had been." she moaned over and over.

Soon after the call ended, people waltzed in and began to reset the room. A little annoyed that they'd rest the room but awed at their speed, Ôffiôñg looked on. Suspecting she would be able to get help with the people milling around, she groped around for something she could use to send a message. For a long time, she skulked around until her feet struck something. She bent down to pick it; it was slender and cold, probably metal. Excited that the same restriction didn't bind it, she darted in all directions until she came in contact with something.

"Who did that? Who was that?" a weak and distant feminine voice asked.

Ôffiôñg wanted to answer but was distracted by the zipping sound and looked up. The tear had reduced again, then it occurred to her that it reduced by the hour, and she had been in the painting for four hours. It would explain why the people in the room were moving fast. Also, her skin had begun to itch like it did when she didn't lather her skin with cream. She also noticed that there was no smell around her. Afraid, she hesitantly blew air into her hand, felt nothing, and questions began to fight for consort in her mind.

What happens when there is no moisture? Am I alive or dead? How do I get out of here? If I made a call to my aunt, would she get it?

Ôffiôñg shuddered. Her phone was in her bag in the corner of the front room with everything else. She was supposed to have gone home as her aunt instructed, but no, she had to look at the painting once more; it swallowed her instead. She tried not to think of woes of similar incidents seen in movies, even though she had seen none where someone was eaten up by a painting. She shuddered at the thought of being eaten up.

Ôffiôñg reprimanded herself for thinking of horrible things and began to pace around her little circle of a dark prison. She had to get out as soon as possible. She started to slide the slender thing again when light surrounded her. She spun and saw countless people come towards her forming a crescent around her; some she recognised from staring at the painting.

"The doorway!" the feminine voice spoke again; this time, the voice, still weak, boomed around her. Its owner was a little taller than a pygmy, in a navy-blue dress and shiny yellow hair. It was the woman who seemed to be in every room.

"What's the cacophony?" a deep, raspy voice groaned, and the group parted to let its owner through. She heard dragging until he was close. He was stick-thin and tall; his moustache reminded her of Hercule Poirot; his hair was the colour of the sand by the beach and ragged; he wore a safari suit, goggles and flippers. A woman in a silk dressing gown and eye mask headband followed him closely.

"Tippins, that!" the man in the safari suit, flippers and goggles said and pointed at the tear in the painting.

A man with a grimace and an eyepatch walked towards her, towering over her to get the thing in her hand; it was a ruler. The man folded the ruler until it looked like a hook and then unhooked a lasso from his belt, knotted them together, twirled it around. Everyone swayed and ducked as he swung it. Finally, he flung it. It neatly latched into the tear, and he is achievement was followed by gasps, cheers, whistles, and applauds.

"Well done," the man in a safari suit, flippers and goggles mumbled and turned to face her, his arms folding across his chest and his fingers drumming his chin.

"How did you get in here?"

"I don't know," Ôffiôñg started and grimaced.

Her skin itched even more.

"You'll get used to the tightness. Best not to scratch," the man in a safari suit, flippers and goggles said and gestured to some of the people who looked like unfinished drawings, then waved his hand for her to continue.

"I cleaned it and tried to catch it."

"It fell?"

"Yes."

"How could it have -"

"Well, I picked it up and placed and then I saw a tear and –"

"You what?" the tiny woman exclaimed, clutching her chest.

"Hold it!" a guttural voice echoed around them, and the people parted to let a man with a limp walk forward. He leaned on a cane when he got to her. He looked exactly like Marcus Harcourt Pepple, the new boy in school that she had been crushing on. He'd only joined her school last month, but he was always around the governor's daughter.

"You got in," the man mumbled, then looked at her. "How did you get in?"

"I—"

The man in a safari suit, flippers and goggles leaned forward and whispered. "Don't answer that. He is thinking."

The man with the cane wasn't the only one thinking because the others murmured, gasped, nodded and shrugged in unison with him.

Ôffiôñg was baffled at the mass in the picture. She was certain the actual house couldn't take a quarter of the people she was seeing in it.

"What's your name?" the tiny woman asked softly.

"Ôffiôñg."

"Odd name," the tiny woman murmured and began to walk around her.

Ôffiôñg frowned at the woman and tried to move, but the space seemed to have reduced as she could no longer extend her hands.

"True," the man in a safari suit, flippers and goggles mumbled, still tapping his chin as he began to pace around her from the opposite direction. "Where are we?"

Ôffiôñg shrugged. "Port Harcourt."

"At a port, that nice," the tiny woman spat, stopped pacing and stared at the man leaning on a cane.

"Now, now, Mrs Cambridge," the man with the limp said with a dismissive wave and raised his brows at Ôffiôñg, "What year is this?"

"2021," Ôffiôñg retorted, her brows raised

defiantly.

"I beg your pardon," the man in a safari suit, flippers and goggles, halted and peered at her. The others either laughed or shook their head simultaneously.

"Mmm," Ôffiôñg mumbled to herself. She didn't know what their expression meant or why the tiny woman looked frightened.

"Now, now Mrs Cambridge." The man on the cane shook his hand as if he was calming a child. "There's still a chance."

"Two thousand and twenty-one. It's Christmas eve," she responded when he asked again.

"Everyone! A party is afoot. There I say, we just might make it," the man in a safari suit, flippers, and goggles exclaimed and clasped his hands excitedly.

He barely finished speaking before the crowd dissipated.

"Tippins!" the man in a safari suit, flippers and goggles cried, pointing at the tear.

Tippins tugged at the rope, widening the gap.

Mrs Cambridge stared intently at Ôffiôñg.

"Get her out," the man in a safari suit, flippers and goggles said.

Mrs Cambridge sneered at Ôffiôñg.

The man in a safari suit, flippers and goggles

whispered: "She might be the key."

"Key. What key?" Ôffiôñg asked, worried and confused.

"The key to getting us out of here," the man in a safari suit, flippers and goggles, responded and padded out of the room.

"How are you here?" Ôffiôñg asked, suddenly suspicious.

Mrs Cambridge scoffed and asked, "You want to leave here?"

"Ehen nawh!" Ôffiôñg grimaced.

Mrs Cambridge raised a brow at her and freed her.

"Yes."

"When you go out, you must make someone like you enough to want to see you again."

"Abasi mmi!" Ôffiôñg exclaimed. No one liked her enough. If her schoolmates didn't boo her for smelling of palm kernel oil, it would be for the smell of camphor in her uniforms.

"Well?" the tiny woman asked already out of the room, which was the exact replica of the real one except that it had no walls.

Ôffiôñg hesitated.

"Only vain people and invisible people get trapped in these paintings. You need a bit of unselfish to get you out. Once every year, we get out to try. We haven't been able to in over a hundred years. Today is that day, and we're far behind schedule."

Ôffiôñg looked longingly at the opening. The party was about to start. She had no one, knew no one who would like her, much less knew her that would be at the party, but she needed to leave this place. Seeing and feeling everything and not being able to be part of it was like being a statue.

She frowned.

Did statues go through this?

Mrs Cambridge exhaled heavily. "You can try to be happy. We have work to do if you don't want to get stuck in here forever. And no, statues don't have flesh and blood or -"

Ôffiôñg gasped, wondering how the woman knew what she was thinking.

Mrs Cambridge chuckled lightly. "The longer you're in here, the more uniform your thought."

Ôffiôñg cringed, gulped, and sheepishly followed the woman to what looked like a dormitory. As they prepped her and themselves, they told her a part of history she'd never heard, like the invention of the draw bridge, of a fish peacemaker, how women sold their daughters for the highest bidder at balls, why the dowry fell on the bride's family in England and how most of them got trapped in the painting.

From their stories, it was believed that the painting was created by the daughter of a wealthy man who was made to marry a man with a fortified castle, a drawbridge and a moat. She was the fairest and most beautiful girl from the village, and even though she was married, men still sought after her. For fear of another stealing her from him, he locked her in the parapet of his tower. It was believed that she used her tears to mix colours and, in the process, created a curse. Her paintings were not burnt down with the castle because she gave them to her mother, whom she only got to see on the eve of Christmas.

Ôffiôñg was curious about the boy that had managed to escape the picture a hundred and twenty years ago. If he left the painting, then she stood a chance too. She worried for them and herself; she wasn't hopeful about meeting someone at the party. They'd been waiting for the key to leave the painting. She should never have touched the paintings.

"You look lovely," the woman who had used an eye mask as headband gushed. She was

wearing a sun-coloured brocade gown.

Not long after, they clamoured into the room she'd come in.

"Ready?"

No one said a word, but she felt a rush as if someone brushed her whole body in one stroke.

"Ladies first," Ellen, who'd earlier had an eye mask headband, was in a sun-coloured gown, said and moved forward.

Tippins stopped her.

"Not in here!" the man with a cane stepped forward and stood beside Tippins, then the man in a safari suit, flippers and goggles joined him. His hair was now pasted to his skull, and he was wearing a monkey jacket.

"Baggins," Ellen exclaimed. "You discarded the flippers and the goggles too."

Baggins nodded then winked at Ôffiôñg. "Why don't we let the last in, out first?"

Ôffiôñg's exit wasn't the same as her entry. She could feel her pores open to take in air and was desperately thirsty. She leaned over the table, now covered with food, to get to the water. Unable to feel her legs, she grabbed the jug, slid to the floor and took the jug to her mouth. She didn't stop until it was empty, then set the jug down before good manners kicked in.

"Ôffiôñg."

Ôffiôñg stiffened, suspecting that someone had caught her. Apprehensively, she turned slowly to face the owner of the voice and found it was her crush, Marcus. She wished the ground could open up and swallow her when she recalled she still had the jug.

"I thought I recognised you," he said.

"Good evening, Marcus," she stammered.

"Good evening. I'm glad you're here. What are you doing down there?"

Not seeing the jug she'd been holding, Ôffiôñg glanced around; she hadn't moved, so how did it get to the table?

"Wow! You look great!"

Ôffiôñg smiled.

"I assumed you didn't like parties. You never attend them."

Ôffiôñg shrugged.

"Anytime I want to talk to you, you disappear."

Ôffiôñg raised a brow. *Did she?*

Marcus scratched the back of his head and then tucked his hands in his pockets. Baggins gave her a thumbs-up right after he'd shoved her into Marcus. Pulling back, she stumbled, but Marcus caught her.

Ôffiôñg curiously glanced around; there was no one close to her.

"Maybe we should go outside," Marcus suggested.

Ôffiôñg, not waiting for him, lifted the front of a dark blue ballgown, walked briskly towards the exit and got stuck in the doorway. She fought to get out. In her struggle, she fell out of the dress's skirt and tumbled down the hilly part of the garden. She struck something and stopped moving. She opened her eyes and squinted at the gown near her head. It was similar to hers, but she hadn't seen the woman before. The woman's hair was the colour of the moon and Tippins' height.

"I leave you for a moment and –"

When she realised it was Mrs Cambridge, she opened her mouth to explain but found her scurrying away.

"Ôffiôñg, are you okay?" Marcus asked as he ran to her side.

She nodded, then recalled falling out of a dress and lowered her head; the dress was still on her, but its ballness was gone, without the number of skirts beneath; it looked every other evening dress but on the garish side.

"That was quite a tumble. I'm sure your taekwondo lessons had nothing to do with it." Marcus said with a smile.

Ôffiôñg eyed him suspiciously. "How did you know I - ?"

"Don't be angry?"

Ôffiôñg's eyes were raised as she waited for an explanation.

"I've sort of been looking for a way to talk to you since I joined your school. Actually, I changed schools to be closer to you."

"You can do that?" Ôffiôñg asked in surprise.

"I did nag my father to get it. He felt I was already in a better one."

"Chai!" *Some people are living large o!*

"I'm so embarrassed."

"Chai!" *All he had to do was nag.*

"I'm sorry, it's just – "

"Chai!" *If it's me that nagged, I know I would see my ears with my eyes.*

"It was the only way I could be close to you."

"Chai!" *Money is good o!*

"You're angry."

"Eh!" she said in a high-pitched voice, blinking.

"You're angry."

"I'm not angry o!"

"Do you want to go out with me, say next week?"

Ôffiôñg frowned at him. It hadn't occurred to her that she was no longer exhausted until then.

"Yes, why not?" Unable to help herself, she asked, "Why do you have so many paintings in your house?"

"What paintings?" he asked, taking her hand in his as he helped her up.

Ôffiôñg inhaled sharply when she glanced at their linked hands; hers were pale. Thinking it was the light, she ignored it. She was with Marcus around the amoeba-shaped lake, the itching started again, and she glanced at her hands; they were already peeling like weathered books in the harmattan wind. She jumped at the sound of popping and withdrew her hands.

"It's only fireworks. They start it five minutes earlier," Marcus explained and gestured.

Five minutes!

With less than five minutes left, desperation kicked in. Ôffiôñg slanted her and noticed that most of the people in the painting had faded. She remembered Mrs Cambridge's words and Marcus hadn't asked to see her again, which made her want to cry.

Impatiently, Ôffiôñg asked, "Do you really like me?"

"Of course," Marcus retorted with raised brows.

"Would you like to see me on Christmas Day?"

"You're cold," Marcus said and offered her his jacket, then sat beside her. "I'll be seeing you on Christmas Day."

"What!?" Ôffiôñg asked, confused. She could see her legs and tucked her hands in the sleeve of her dress.

"Christmas is in less than five minutes."

Ôffiôñg instinctively bit her finger, but there was nothing to bite. She glanced in the shadows and saw Baggins urging her on.

"I would like to ask you out, but I'm afraid you might say no," Marcus mumbled and toyed with his fingers.

Ôffiôñg fumed. Far ahead, she saw her aunt looking around, worried, and the will to live kicked in. Her aunt may not be her best friend, but she was family. She couldn't afford to remain in a painting, in 2D forever. She looked longingly at Marcus and asked, "How will you know if you don't ask me?"

"Will you say no?"

"You haven't asked," Ôffiôñg mumbled, her

voice weaker.

"Will you say yes?"

"Ask already," Ôffiôñg sternly urged, her voice wobbled and dwindled.

"Will you go out with me on Christmas Day?"

Marcus nodded. "Yes, I will."

Ôffiôñg felt a sharp pain as she instinctively gulped air; she was breathing. The colourful light popped in the sky in sparkling splinters. While Marcus turned to the sound, Ôffiôñg stared at her hands and watched life return to them. She shrugged his jacket off and let the cold breeze encase her. Cold air never felt so good.

"Thank you," she heard in the breeze that twirled in front of her and dispersed. It was Baggins.

"Stay away from my paintings," Mrs Cambridge's voice echoed in a shriller voice around her.

"I didn't hear your response," Marcus mumbled.

"What?" Ôffiôñg asked distractedly.

"Will you go out with me on Christmas Day?"

Ôffiôñg's chest swelled painfully. She arched her back and exhaled sharply; her ears felt like it was filled with water. She could smell moss and damp rotting grass. She was breathing. She

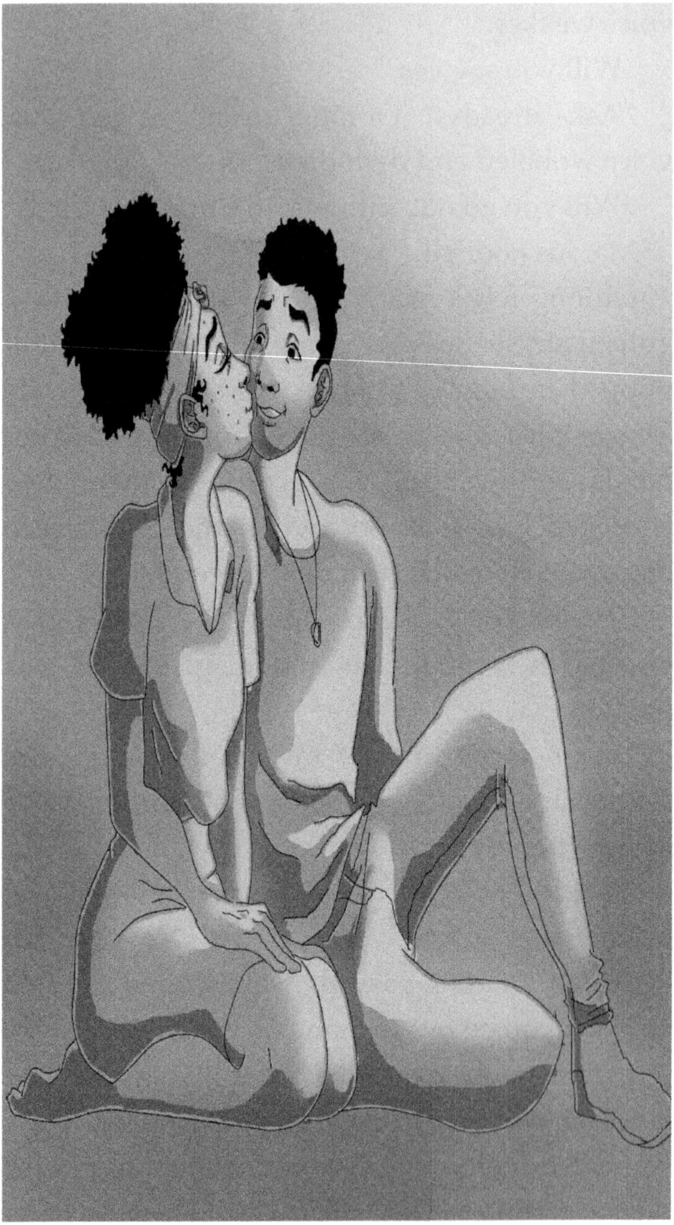

scrubbed her arm. She could feel. Tears were in her eyes as she let out a relieved sigh. "It's Christmas Day."

"Yes, it is. But –"

"What about the governor's daughter?" Ôffiôñg asked, getting up and kicking off her sandals to feel the grass under her feet.

"Former governor's daughter, you mean. What about her?"

"I thought you were an item," Ôffiôñg mumbled and brushed her feet over the grass, one after the other.

"What?" Marcus guffawed. "She's my neighbour."

He pointed at the house opposite them. "It used to be the outhouse over a hundred years ago."

"It definitely was," Ôffiôñg said before she could stop herself.

"Do you want a history lesson?"

"I think I've had enough history lessons," Ôffiôñg retorted quickly.

Marcus exhaled heavily. "I'm so happy you said that. Everyone else seems to want to story."

They sat by the pond and watched the sunrise. Never in her wildest dreams would she have admired such a sight. But then, never in her wildest dream did she expect to end up in a painting for almost ten hours.

"Marcus Harcourt Pepple," she mumbled and planted a kiss on his cheek. "Merry Christmas."

"Merry Christmas," Marcus retorted with a chuckle and touched his cheek.

Ôffiôñg observed Marcus for a while and smiled and made a promise to make no more wishes.

"Ôffiôñg!"

Ôffiôñg jumped to her feet at her aunt's voice and offered Marcus an apologetic smile.

Agnes Kay-E is a Nigerian author based in England and the author of eight books, including Blossom in Winter, a bestseller. She writes contemporary fiction of vast genres, fantasy, and new age fiction. Her latest is Anatomy of Harmony. She is presently working on another Contemporary Fiction. In her spare time, she sings and writes music.

A BLACK MAN'S DILEMMA

David Eke

I watched Papa leave that day till he disappeared from my sight, as usual, with suspicion in every word that proceeded from his lips and despise for the way he walked because it perfectly told who he was. He'd tell us:

"Do good at school, kids."

Next, he'd peck me and my brother on our cheeks, hug and kiss Mama on her lips, and walk so boyishly and swaggeringly out of the house. Mama would also stand and watch with us - me and my brother, Derrick. We'd stand where we were, in the parlour for long minutes, and watch his movement till we lost sight of him. We looked through the window, down the end of Christen Street. Our ugly house ended the long street.

Papa's trousers were always baggy, and his shirts same. He wore chain necklaces, fake ones. He loved them just as much as he loved his plaited hair. Whenever I'd try to loosen one, on those nights we were lucky to have him at home, he'd stop me with a scold. My eyes always tightened and produced tears, all in an attempt to get him to carry me in his arms and pamper me. He always did.

"Hope you have everything in your bags?" Mama asked, interrupting our state. We were used to that question, so whenever she asked, we intuitively said yes, even when we didn't have our school notes in our bags or had forgotten the three slices of bread Mama usually packed for our lunch in the kitchen. Luckily, we hadn't forgotten anything that day, or so I thought.

There had been a time when Derrick forgot his three slices of bread. He came to me, in my small class. It had been time for lunch break. He whispered into my ear.

"Can you give me some bread?"

I looked at him from head to toe, mouth shut, but eyes squinted for a while. I saw how much we looked alike, and that was nothing new. We were twins, but he was minutes older, that's if the idea that the first child that comes out is older is true.

I looked at his school uniform shorts. He was still wearing shorts. He was growing very tall; we were growing very tall. His whole uniform was rumpled; more rumpled than mine. There was no iron at home; hardly any power as well, so we

wore our uniform like that. He was in Grade 5 then, and I was in Grade 7. I wore skirts, unlike his class girls that still wore pinafore gowns. We were meant to be in the same class, but he had failed his entrance exams and had to repeat the class because Mama and Papa didn't have the money to afford another school. That was why he still wore shorts and not trousers, like my class boys did.

He kicked my leg lightly, reminding me he was there.

"What?" I ended up asking.

"Please sisi." He said, pouting. I couldn't bear seeing him like that. I didn't actually want to give him some bread. Why'd I even? Three slices of bread were barely enough. That's what Mama and Papa could afford: a small loaf. We'd eat 4 slices of bread each in the morning with homemade orange juice. Almost tasteless, it was, but what could we do? The orange tree, planted by someone we didn't know, was our greatest possession, I believe.

'Why are you so careless?' I wanted to ask Derrick. But my class boys and girls would have heard me. Cindy, the only white girl in class, would have asked me what happened. We all knew how nosy she loved to be. She didn't live in our neighbourhood, though, so I always wondered why she was in the town school. Only her and another boy in Grade 10 were white. Why they chose to attend our school, I didn't know. I motioned for Derrick to bend, and I whispered into his ear:

"It's in my bag, on the shelf. Take all. I'm not hungry." All eyes were on us. Maybe they admired how close to me, and my brother seemed, or they were wondering why he was in our class.

He smiled, whispered thank you to me, and moved quickly to the back of the whole class. He knew my bag. It was small and recklessly torn in different parts. The Cinderella design that was once there had been peeled by Derrick, and only the shape of her face and gown remained. He walked out of the class, trying not to make any noise with the Ziploc bag containing the three slices of bread without butter - butter was too expensive. He placed it against his stomach as he walked out of class. Only my form teacher must have seen what he came to take, our regular lunch. We had the worst lunch in the town school, and I'm sure of it. That day, I was so hungry, but I'd do anything for my twin brother. Well, as a result of my hunger experience that day, I didn't ever let him forget his lunch.

We stepped out of the house and waited in the front while Mama locked the door. That usually took ten minutes, but that day, it had taken five thereabout. The lock was broken, and Mama had to keep turning and turning the key before it brought out the two big nuts. Opening was usually no easier, but we'd managed. Mama and the priest at church had done a great job in teaching us to be contented.

"Mama, let me help." Derrick would normally offer, but he didn't that morning. He just stared vaguely at Mama in her everyday gown with faded flowery designs. I was looking at him. Maybe he had the bad feeling I was having that day, as well.

We started our walk to school, taking Gloris Street, on the right direction. It was just as long as Christen Street. We all held each other's hands, as we walked.

"Derrick lead us in prayer," Mama said. I wondered why we didn't just do it in the parlour like we did on Saturdays. How long did it take that Mama thought it best for it to be done on the road? Well, the Bible said, 'Pray without ceasing'. Derrick prayed his short and filled with grammatical blunders. God could see the heart, so that wasn't a problem.

I watched Mama's face as we walked. She always had a smile on and then those big sunglasses. Even when it was cloudy, she had those big glasses. I think they gave her confidence because her widest smiles came with them, revealing brown teeth. We didn't always brush our teeth. Mama wasn't a fan of the charcoal and salt we had to use sometimes, so she always stayed days till Papa came with toothpaste from wherever he came from.

As we walked, she exchanged greetings with everyone, including the white woman who had called her a chimpanzee one day in the grocery shop out of town. I had followed her that day, and as I watched her face the floor of the shop after receiving such a word from that white woman, I felt enraged. I wished I wasn't so small so I could at least slap that woman and tell her we were just as human. But Mama didn't bear any grudge. She was a Christian, and I adhered to her every word.

Derrick always fed his eyes with the flashy cars that drove past us, looking back at them as they speedily fled away. He'd call at me, then say:

"Look at that one. It's a new model Lamborghini. I must buy one of those."

I looked back because he wanted me to. They

actually never interested me, and they just got me wondering what their owners were looking for, passing a town like ours. Mama, as usual, looked down at us, tiny minions, compared to her, who was very tall, and said:

"Yes, and even bigger ones."

"Amen!" We both exclaimed in unison.

We got closer to school, and Mama stopped at her usual place of stoppage. It was like our own parking lot or walking lot, if you may. We still had to walk about one hundred meters, before getting to the school's brown gate. It was one of the only schools with a gate in our area. The look behind that gate was just like that of our house, although we didn't have a gate.

There was just a shabby building, partly made of wood, like our house, having classes divided by boards used for teaching and a small lawn with bushes they called flowers. I personally knew the gate was there to shield my eyes from the appalling look of our school. I also knew Mama didn't stop one hundred meters away because she was rushing to get to her place of work, where she worked as a babysitter for many kids.

I knew it was because of her gown and the weird-looking cheap slippers. I knew it was because she didn't match up to other parents, who wore makeup and shiny lip gloss. They weren't doing so well, too, but she didn't want to let them know ours was the worst. Even though she never said these, I knew.

Derrick and I continued walking the remaining distance together. He was taller than me, just a bit, though. Mama watched us from where she stopped. The little one-hundred meters felt like a thousand that day, and the thousands from our house felt like millions. This was after a police car drove speedily from behind us and parked in front of our school. We always arrived at school late, so everyone was already in.

The only people out and watching were the other blacks living in our tight neighbourhood, busy with their cleaning routines. A policeman, the one who had been driving, jumped out of the driver's seat. He was white and had red spots all over his face. He was huge, much huger than Papa. The second policeman came out as well, from the back seat this time. He was smallish but white. My brother and I stood and witnessed how hastily the policemen were coming out. I don't think Mama had noticed. When I looked back, she was crossing the road to the other diversion.

"Papa!" Derrick screamed.

I looked in the direction of the police car again. They were both dragging handcuffed Papa out of their car. He was struggling with them. I knew Papa wouldn't let them win. Derrick shouted 'Papa!' again and ran to where they had started hitting Papa. He was on the ground. I couldn't run to him. I don't know why. I stood where I was. Mama screamed. I heard her voice, from behind. She was with them in less than 10 seconds. I didn't know Mama could run that fast. Seeing Mama there, I ran to join them.

"Please, officers, stop. Please stop," Mama pleaded.

The men weren't listening. The huge policeman raised Papa from the ground and hit him on the car's bonnet. The smallish one placed his little pestle on his head.

"Please, uncle. Please, sir…" Derrick had started begging.

I joined in.

"Please let Papa be."

Other black folks in the neighbourhood, mostly women and children, were watching, holding to poles for comfort while they witnessed what they were used to seeing, what we were used to seeing. They must have told their husbands to run or hide, that the police were around. That was our own day. I knew our own day would come. Everyone had their own judgment day. I just didn't know we had lesser time till ours.

"Where's your son, huh?" the smallish policeman asked Papa.

"Look at him. Let me be!" Papa was still being resistant.

"Why do you want my son?" Mama asked and held Derrick's shoulder, drawing him to her body as if capable of protecting him from the bullets in the policeman's gun. He wasn't shying away. He was looking at them. I don't know if his heart was pounding like mine. I don't know if he didn't feel like crying at the sight of that gun on Papa's head.

"How old is your son, woman?" the smallish policeman asked.

"He's just twelve. Please don't hurt him," Papa said.

"Shut up," the huge policeman said and hit Papa's back very heavily with his fist. Papa wailed in pain, his face still on the car's bonnet.

"We didn't ask you. How old is your son, woman?" the huge policeman asked.

"He's twelve. My husband isn't lying. Please let him be," Mama said. She wasn't with her sunglasses anymore. Her eyes were red, ready to produce tears. I'm sure she wished she could kill those men. Who would take care of us if they took her husband away? I'm sure she was already wondering.

"I'm so sorry, officer. Please let my family be. I'm the one you want. Please!" Papa had started begging. I didn't like that he was begging. I wanted him to continue being resistant. But what could he do? Hearing Papa beg increased the intensity of our pleas. Mama went on her knees. We followed suit. I heard the noise of our school gate. It was being locked from inside.

"Young man, are you involved with any drugs?" The smallish policeman asked Derrick.

"Sir…" Derrick was trying to say.

"How'd you think such a little child would have drugs?" Papa asked. I saw his hands were shaking. I could see his underwear. It was the normal one, white and, just like all his clothing possessions, baggy.

"Let the man speak for himself."

"He's twelve, only twelve. Please let us be." Mama said.

I looked at Derrick. Why was he looking at the ground? Why had he recoiled? Why had he stopped begging and looking bold? We needed bold him at the moment. Why was he holding back?

"Shuu!" The smallish policeman called out to Derrick. He looked up.

"I'll ask for the last time. Are you with any drugs?"

"Answer, baby," Mama said to him. Mama had begun to cry. She couldn't hold it back anymore. I wanted to cry, too, but I didn't think that was what Papa needed. He wasn't crying, so I didn't cry.

"If I tell the truth, will you let Papa be?" Derrick let out. What was wrong with him? I was expecting a straight 'No'. I'm sure everyone else, including the policemen, too. What was he saying? The two men looked at each other, smiled and nodded.

"Deal, young man," the smallish policeman said. Mama had stopped crying for a second. Papa had stopped struggling. I had stopped myself from moving my knees because of the pain I felt around them.

"I have some," Derrick said.

Mama was quick to speak. "What are you saying, son? Tell them! Tell them you are joking. Or do you mean the painkillers I bought days ago? No, they are not talking of that. Tell them, please, baby," Mama was saying. She started crying again.

I looked at Papa. He wasn't moving. I hoped he hadn't died of the shock. I was a bit relieved when he raised his head and turned it in the other direction.

"Fuck. Fuck..." he started saying quietly.

"Come and show us, young man," The smallish policeman said and took Derrick's hand.

"You won't take my son nowhere," Mama said, holding Derrick's other hand.

"Then you'll come with us, I guess," the wicked man said.

He let go of Derrick's hand. Mama held Derrick tight, asking him more questions in whispers. It started seeming like they had all forgotten I was there. I was still looking at Papa. I think he was crying. He had pushed his lips backwards. I hadn't seen any tears yet, but his eyes were closed. The smallish policeman took a phone from his pocket and dialled a number.

"Unit five-o-seven, come over here! The trash just became heavier," he said into the phone.

I hadn't been surprised by Derrick's answer. I was only surprised he said it. I thought he had promised to stop. I thought he had promised to put all of it away. For real, what was he doing? Did he really believe the policemen? I had caught him sniffing on a whitish powder-like substance one day. That was the one they called cocaine.

I had woken up that afternoon, and I went to the kitchen to get water. I was surprised when I didn't see him beside me when I woke up. We normally observed siesta by that time, 3 pm, when Mama went out to where only she knew she was going. She never told us. She'd only say, 'I'd be back, babies', then walk out of the house with her small red bag. That was the bag she was carrying.

When I got to the kitchen, I stopped by the door. I watched Derrick do what he was doing for about a minute. He was sniffing on cocaine, standing but bending a little to get his nose and tongue on the powder-like substance. I was alarmed. My eyes and palm became wet. When I called his name, he jumped.

"What are you doing?" I asked him in a low voice.

"Please don't let Mama know or Papa." He started saying, almost in tears himself. I was confused then. I thought the drugs made people do crazy things. How come he was calm and regretful? Maybe he had just started sniffing on it when I got there.

"I won't, but what are you doing?" I asked

him, although I knew what he was doing.

"I'm sorry. It's something bad. I won't do it again. I promise! I'll throw it all away," he said. I could read he was truly sorry from his face. The white dust was on his nose and lips.

"Okay. Why? And please throw it away."

"It calms me, but I won't take it anymore."

He poured it into the sink and pushed the tap on. He threw the white waterproof into the bin.

"Derrick, what's the problem?" I asked him. I was his younger sister, but to be honest, I felt older than him, most of the time. He began to cry. I moved and hugged him.

"I'm sorry. I just miss Papa. Why can't he play and stay with us like Brandon's parents do?"

"But he does play with us," I said.

"Yeah… once in a year. I want him here. Mama tries, but she isn't enough. They always mock me in class. They also talk of their fathers, but I can't talk about mine."

I didn't have any words for him again. I just hugged him tighter and kept saying, 'sorry'. I hadn't seen him with drugs in the last year, but I still had my suspicions. Hearing him give that answer affirmed my suspicions but shocked me because the brother I had and knew always kept his promises. And if he had fallen back on this promise, he'd not be so naïve to believe the policeman's offer. It was what shocked me that he gave in to the man's offer.

Another police car arrived in a bit. Papa still hadn't made another attempt at resisting. Mama was still holding her son. The policemen were restraining Papa, and I was there, doing nothing, not being counted.

We were led into the second police car while Papa entered the back seat of the police car where he had been. The smallish policeman had his gun on Papa's head and sat beside Papa in the back seat. I kept looking at him, wondering what he'd do if he mistakenly pulled the trigger. They could just drop Papa on the road, bleeding and dying and push us out of the car to mourn his insignificant death. He didn't matter after all; to them, we didn't matter! I didn't know our house was far from our school till that day. Worry and anxiety really made time passage slow.

As we got to our shabby looking house that I was so ashamed to let people know I lived in, the policemen climbed out very speedily. I wondered if that was how they were trained to come out of cars. Mama gently came out with Derrick. She had been carrying him on her lap throughout the suddenly long journey. I think it was the

speediness of my heartbeat that made other things slow to me. I climbed out fully ready for our house's overhauling. What would happen next? I kept asking myself. Would Papa be taken away? And did Derrick still have drugs? I walked in front of him and Mama, so I could get to whatever position his drugs were in and remove it before him. There were six white policemen with us in the house, and they all had guns except the hugest one. I was almost peeing on my pants.

The policemen didn't need Mama or Papa to open the door. It was another criminal black family, so they kicked the door open. I was only surprised at how easily the door opened, only with one kick. They were inside our home in a bit, ransacking, scattering, opening, eroding our privacies. I watched them. Papa was on the floor in the parlour, held down by the macho man. Mama and Derrick were inside our room. I was there in the parlour, standing and watching.

"Found!" A policeman shouted from the kitchen and started coming out. I could hear his heavy footsteps. My heart tripped into my stomach. I didn't move, so I'd not become a suspect too. Two men were searching the parlour. I was a bit happy. At least, no one had seen anything in me and Derrick's room.

"Good. Search for more." The smallish one said. What made him believe there was more? What did he take us for?

"There's nothing in the room." The ones in the room, said as they came out with Derrick. Obviously, he wasn't going to show them where his drugs were anymore. Mama must have told him a lot in the car. Her whispers were the most quiet, so the police didn't even notice she was speaking with him.

"Young man, where are your drugs?" The smallish one asked, remembering Derrick's confession. Papa turned his head to Derrick. Probably, he, too, had forgotten Derrick confessed. Derrick was looking at him. He began to cry, fear written all over his facial expression. He couldn't hold it no more. Papa was crying too, and this time, the tears had rolled down. He looked away from Derrick, who was facing the rugged floor.

The smallish policeman drew Derrick from Mama and pointed his pestle at her, so she wouldn't fight back for her son. He motioned for one of them to hold Mama, and they did. I was praying to the Almighty in my heart. I needed him to rescue us from those monsters, but I later saw it was our own wage for our sins. The smallish, and conspicuously the most evil, policeman placed his gun on little Derrick's head and asked him again. Derrick must have been frightened out of this world. I was already in space because of fear, myself. They could actually shoot him, and nothing would have happened. No one would have petitioned the policemen for shooting someone without legal proof of a crime. No one would have taken on our case. We were nothing!

"It's in the kitchen," Derrick said, in between quiet sobs.

"Is it this, young man?" The policeman from the kitchen asked, raising a small white pack of cocaine in a transparent bag.

"Yes," he said and looked down again.

"Where had it been?" The smallish policeman asked. I looked at his evil face. So that was the way they used to fish out more drugs!

"Under the dustbin," Derrick's little teenage mouth muttered.

"Correct sergeant?" the beast asked to confirm.

"Yes, sir."

"Okay. Let's flush this trash," Mama screamed and fell on the floor at that pronouncement. She still didn't come to me to tell me it'll be fine. She crawled to the feet of the most evil policeman.

"Please forgive my boy. It's not his fault. Please." That was when I started thinking for myself. Where had Derrick seen the drugs in the first place? We didn't go out, unlike other black kids in the hood given so much freedom. We were always indoors or on the lawn. When could he have gotten it from someone if he did?

"Mama, forgive me. Papa, please forgive me." Derrick was saying.

"No, boy. It's my mistake…" Papa started. The policeman on him seemed to have had a bit of sympathy and let him stand.

"You'll be going to the juvenile, you little man." The evil man uttered, pulling at Derrick's shirt. I was still there, standing aloof. Papa continued talking. His hands had been let free. The macho policeman wasn't so cruel after all. He let Papa get to Derrick. Papa hugged Derrick very tight. I wanted a hug too. Was Derrick being given all the attention for being a bad child? What of me? Papa held his chin and spoke, tears trickling down his face. I had never seen Papa in such a state.

"This is all my fault. I've always wanted a better life for you two, but this is what it came to." That was when he remembered I existed, and he tugged at my shoulders, held me towards his sides, and kissed my forehead.

"I became this because of my father, and he was that because of his father." Papa was talking slowly. Mama was looking at him, still crying but folding her lips in a kind of admiration. What had attracted her to Papa in the first place? Derrick had told me they had us after a series of failed abortions, so they had to get married.

"I'm sorry for failing you all. I'm so sorry. There's no way to put the little food I put on our table in this community of ours, without doing this. We don't matter to the white folks. They be living large, but it's fine. It has come to this, and I can't take it no more." My eyes were on Mama; she was furrowing her brows after his touching words. Papa pushed me and Derrick away from him. He reached for the smallish policeman's gun and ended it.

I heard two loud shots, and Papa fell on the floor. His eyes were open. He fell slowly. He had shot his head. He knew how to handle a gun.

Mama was the first to react. She jumped on her husband. She kept pushing his chest as if it'd rewind life and stop Papa from what he had just done. Derrick and I cried; we cried so bitterly, quietly. Mama began to roll at some point, opening her legs, and then the evil policeman,

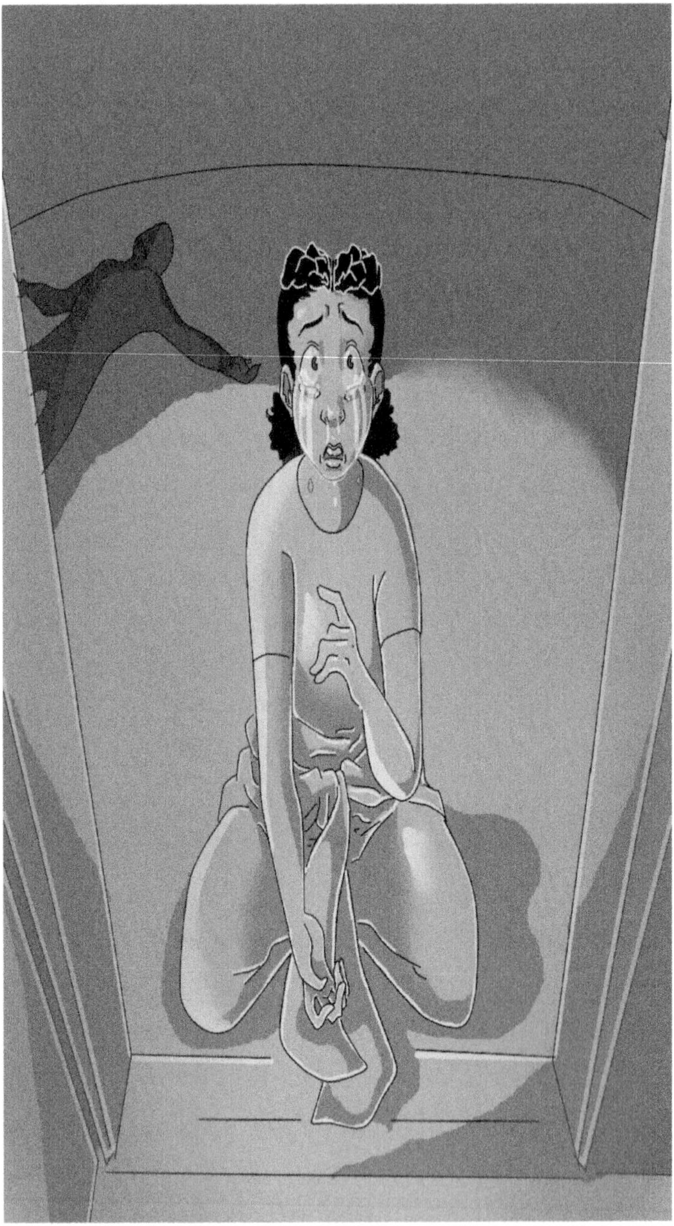

with no remorse, spotted a pack of drugs carefully tied to her lap.

I was shocked. We were shocked. Mama was a Christian, a very good one. Could she do that too? I remember her last words to me, as they all left me that day:

"Baby, this is the true life of a black person. Papa and I did all this to get food. We needed food; you needed food. I'm sure Derrick got those drugs from

my bag. Please forgive us." They carried them away.

The pain was just too hard to bear. The only person who could have shared it with me was waving at me in tears as he was being carried on the macho man's shoulders. I fell on my knees, staring at Papa's numb face.

How'd I walk this life without them?

David Eke is a Nigerian writer who aims at speaking the underlying truth about power. He seeks to present the many problems we face in our world in beautifully written fiction. He runs a blog which he equally uses to talk about these problems.

ÈGUNGUN

(The Masquerade)

Oluwatoyin M.

The fate of the unseen

Ajibola ran as fast as she could; something was chasing her with a cutlass. Lost and out of breath, she found shelter under a shady tree. She shook her head in the darkness as her heart pounded wildly. She hadn't offended anyone, nor did she borrow money from a person, but she felt a figure in a bright costume was after her dear life. She looked behind to see if what was chasing her had left, but the tree she found comfort in turned out to be a violent predator. In a twinkle of an eye, the big oak tree swallowed her whole…

"Arghhhhh…" Ajibola cried out from her sleep.

Sweat covered her whole body as if she had just bathed. Her whole existence mattered to her. Although she was happy, it was just a nightmare, the recurring nature kept her awake all night. She was scared and needed to talk to someone about it.

The only person she could talk to had been her mother, who had died two years ago. The

relationship between her father was estranged.

She put on soft music as a lullaby to put her to sleep, exhaled sharply and shut her eyes once again.

The alarm woke her up at exactly 6 o'clock. She prepared for work and hoped her nasty boss wouldn't complain anymore. She has just begun her internship at an insurance company in Lagos. Although she lived alone in a one-room apartment, she had gotten herself after she finished school. It had been two years since she visited her hometown in Idanre in Ekiti State. She had never felt welcome and didn't bother as her mother was no more.

Being the only child of her mother, she grew up to receive the love of her mother alone. Her father was never present nor contributed a dime to her life from the start. He believed a female child was useless, and he would only send a male child to school.

Ajibola's mother worked really hard to take good care of her only daughter. She sold all her belongings to send Ajibola to school in the city. She believed education was very important in both male and female children. But when the time came for her to reap the fruit she sowed, death came knocking on her door, taking her away from her beloved.

The death of her mother took a toll on Ajibola; it left her feeling abandoned. She wished death never existed and cursed its existence. She lived in agony and worked her butt off to get the absence of her mother off her mind. Ajibola did all she could to make her deceased mother proud. She knew her mother would be proud of her wherever she was.

Ajibola took on odd jobs to make a living until she secured an internship at the insurance company. Due to her patience and hard work, she was loved by everyone except her boss, Mr Adekitan.

Mr Adekitan was a young CEO who had life easy for him and had climbed the ladder laid for him by his wealthy parents. Being handsome, with dark, beautiful skin looking like it would taste like honey and the charming smile of a child, all the ladies flocked around him, old and young, but his nasty attitude was a turn-off for Ajibola.

The first day Ajibola started working in the company, she fell for his charm, only to discover that he had a nasty attitude; although meticulous about work, he was cold as ice. Ajibola was a charm of the company, and most of her ideas were used to boost sales, but Adekitan would have one or two things to say

to her, even if it was unnecessary.

Mr Adekitan, whose office was tucked into a corner of the building would every morning stand by his window to peer at Ajibola as she steadily typed on her computer. No one had caught up with this behaviour.

A colleague informed her that she had a guest. She was surprised and suspicious because everyone she knew or knew her dwelt in Idanre. Out of curiosity, she went to check.

On her way out, she recalled the nightmare she'd been having, and an intense feeling that something was wrong fell on her, but she just couldn't figure it out.

Outside, three men in suits were waiting for her and greeted her in a chant of incantations and, in a blink, transformed into masquerades. She screamed but no one heard her; it was as if no one had witnessed what she saw.

"*Gbo ikilo arabinrin...mase fi egun sare.* Heed this! Don't joke with this Masquerade," the three chanted and disappeared.

Ajibola stood like a stone in disbelief at what she had witnessed. Sweat covered her body, she shook with fear so much that her vibrating phone frightened her. The warning kept ringing in her ears, and she ran inside to take

cover before picking up her call.

"Helll...hello…" she answered in a low voice, fearing that it was from the masquerades because there was no caller ID.

"Hello...*se eyin ni akobi omo baba dipo*? Are you the first child of Mr Dipo?" the man on the phone replied.

"Eh!?" Ajibola retorted, not recognising the voice.

"*Ara baba yin oya, wa sin reti yin ni ile.* Your father is sick. And he is waiting for you to come home."

She dropped the call since she wasn't interested in her father's case. She thought he had other children, why would he be calling for her?

She forgot about it and was busy with work. At the close of the day, Mr Adekitan offered to take her home in his Porsche, and she accepted.

She forgot about it and was busy with work. At the close of the day, Mr Adekitan offered to take her home in his Porsche, and she accepted.

While Mr Adekitan tapped on his steering wheel and stole glances at Ajibola in the silent car, Ajibola pondered on the nightmare, the strange visitors and the unknown caller and her father and thought of visiting home. She nodded to herself: she would need to go home to solve the mystery. Perhaps visit a *babalawo* who would consult *Ifa*, to solve her problem.

"Sir, can you grant me a favour?" Ajibola asked.

"What is bothering you? Money? Promotion? Fire on, I will do it for you!" Mr Adekitan boasted fiercely, surprising Ajibola.

"Sir! How… Em…" Ajibola cleared her throat. "I want to visit my hometown tomorrow… They called to inform me that my father is very sick. I need to visit home to see him."

Mr Adekitan agreed and began to ask her questions about her father, surprising her further with his concern and insisted on taking her to her hometown but she rejected his offer. After Mr Adekitan insisted, she took the money he offered her for her trip.

The Road to Hell

Ajibola had woken up early to catch a bus to take her to her hometown; she was the first passenger to have arrived. She sat close to a nursing mother whose child wouldn't stop crying, and to her right was a religious man of God who prayed without being asked before the bus took off, a woman sold shea butter to some customers on the bus and the driver who seemed half-drunk and dozed off a little but

regained his consciousness when the whole passengers descended on him. For him to accept his fault was a problem, he cursed out people who tried correcting his ways.

The journey to Idanre from Lagos was just a four-hour journey, but it turned into a lifetime of hell for Ajibola. The traffic was bad, and there was too much heat. The baby beside her kept crying like she hadn't eaten for days, while the confused mother was still in denial of what to do.

Ajibola regretted saying no to Adekitan. She already missed him as if she had known him forever. She would forgive his past actions and make a man out of him, she pondered as she imagined both of them as a couple.

That fantasy distracted her from the trip but was ruined when a man from the back seat poked her from behind. He had been harassing her from behind by touching her buttocks, and she had readjusted her position to free herself from the harassment, but this man wouldn't stop, and since the car seats were as old as forever, she couldn't escape the predator.

Out of anger, she turned around and slapped the man.

Everyone's attention dwelt on the two. Annoyed by what had happened, the man tried defending himself by calling Ajibola names and pointing out the fact that he was older than her, to which everyone started pointing fingers at

Ajibola. Ajibola could not explain what she had experienced so she warned the man.

The journey was once peaceful again but got interrupted when the bus broke down on the express way. They had to wait for the mechanic to arrive to see things for themselves since there wasn't any help the driver could render to fix the bus.

In the heat, passengers complained and whined about their predicament, the baby started crying again, and the child's mother took out a hand fan to make her feel better. The man of God next to Ajibola kept going in and out of the bush to 'free' himself.

Once again, Ajibola regretted not allowing Mr Adekitan to give her a ride home. It was as if he knew Ajibola was thinking about him because Mr Adekitan texted her to ask about her well-being and also to ask if the journey was going peacefully. She replied and was happy that he was worried about her. They both texted each other about how their day was going until the driver returned to continue their journey.

They reached Idanre and left all their worries behind.

The Mandate

Ajibola took a bike from the bus station to her father's house. On the way, she witnessed the festive mood of the local town. Both young and old were wearing happy grins. Out of curiosity,

she asked the bike man what could make the people so excited and calm since she knew her town people were always in a hurry to get things done.

"Odun Egungun Ku ola ni. Tomorrow is the Egungun festival," the bike man replied.

She recalled the masquerades and wondered if it was connected to the festival. Her father's compound was brimming with people she had never met. The strange feeling returned, and she wondered if her father was no more.

Was this why they came?

She loved her father even though they were estranged. She was relieved when she saw her father come out to greet her, unlike before, he would give her a cold shoulder. Her brothers rallied around her like chickens who had just seen their first meal, and her stepmother became all caring and even asked about her trip from Lagos and what she would eat.

Ajibola questioned why her father wasn't in a sick bed, but he brushed it off saying he became well.

As they were discussing, three older men entered their living room. Ajibola recognized them to be the three men who had visited yesterday at her place of work. She was scared to see the men in her house, but her father told her not to be scared since they were there for her.

Why on earth would these three individuals have business with me?

"*Se oti se tan lati wo aso Egun?* Is she ready to wear the garment of the masquerade?"

Ajibola was lost for words. *Eegun.*

"How? Why? What business do I have with Egun?"

Ajibola's father later explained when the men left; the gods of the lands had chosen her to be the next candidate that would wear the masquerade garment and dance around the whole town in order to allow peace to reign in the community.

"What? What is my business with that? I only came home because you asked me to. Why on earth would I dance around in the *Egun* clothes? I am a girl, not a male child?"

There was never in the history of the town that a female child would dance around in any *Egungun* garment. Ajibola thought it was a joke and questioned her father. He pleaded: if she didn't accept the whole town would not have peace, and even their family would not be left out. He begged her to consider the offer, this was the first time he felt proud of his daughter. If Ajibola agrees to the proposal, his whole family will be celebrated in the community.

Night fell as Ajibola still pondered on the ridiculous offer. She is someone from the city who had a life and reputation, why on earth would she be an *Egungun*?

Ajibola fell asleep and dreamt of her

deceased mother urging her to respect the elders. She told her to listen to the gods and never go against her father, for it was her destiny to favour the gods.

She woke up from the scary dream; it was the first time her mother had appeared angrily at her. She knew she couldn't escape her destiny, but a thought came to her to escape at night before morning came. But she couldn't do it, her mother was all she had, so humiliating herself to please her mother was her only choice.

Egungun Festival

Before Ajibola could wear the costume, she was first empowered with some charms to ward off negativity. The priests were proud of her decision, and so was her father. He threw a big party at his house to celebrate his daughter. He was, all of a sudden, a proud father. He was the type that never hoped for a girl child to bring glory to his household, but his only daughter was now making him proud.

The ceremony started as people gathered around to see the miracle; the first female *Egungun*. The first female who would dance around to bless the town. The Kabiyesi also gathered some people of high repute in his palace to await the arrival of the *Egungun* to pass over his palace. It was a once-in-a-lifetime experience for everyone, and no one wanted to miss it.

As planned, she danced in the heavy costume, knowing the dance steps without practice. She enjoyed the praise and felt on top of the world. For the first time in her life she mattered. She was proud of herself and hoped her mother would be likewise.

The Kabiyesi praised her bravery and awarded her a traditional title. She became a role model to every girl child in her town. What life had for her was good intentions, and she was happy she hadn't turn it down.

Oluwatoyin M. is a twenty-three years old Nigerian who's passionate about storytelling. She's driven and motivated by African literature and poetry, and most importantly, loves the element and art of her culture. "Being an African is my identity, and I'm super proud to be a Nigerian," she'd usually say.
She hopes to inspire others to read and explore her imaginative mind.
She also writes about African history, food, lifestyle, and culture for the Afrovibe magazine.

OTHER KEPRESSNG TITLES

Notes on Love
Rebirth
Flip-Flop
Oops!
Bound by Fate
Sink or Swim
Loving Nigeria

CONTACTS

Thank you for purchasing my book.
I hope you enjoyed it.
For more, let's meet at any of these places.

Facebook: https://www.facebook.com/kepressng
Instagram: https://www.instagram.com/kepressng
For newsletters: https://www.kepressng.com

ABOUT US

Kepressng (KEP) Ltd is an African publishing company with a vision to broaden the impact of African literary works and compositions. We aim to remind the world that we're avid readers and to combat the self-imposed superstitions that Africans don't read.

Our core values are Excellence, Collaboration, Discovery, & Generosity.

To mark our official opening, we introduced the **KepressNG Anthology Prize** in 2021—a unique collection of short stories from debut and seasoned authors with African lineage. This multi-collection was founded with the vision of developing and expanding African literature by creating a competition for selecting the best stories.

The KepressNG Anthology prize is designed for teenagers, though not restricted to them, to write stories that they'd love to read. Our stories matter, and who better to tell them than us? Societies evolve, and the most affected is the youth.
Tying submissions to a theme is our way of helping new and emerging authors establish a discipline for telling the story without the faff.

The prose is in short form and not restricted to a specific genre.
There's a belief that short stories are a thing of the past, but most young adults start out with short stories. Should we now abandon them in the abyss or support their growth in literary proficiency?

If you're interested in sponsoring or partnering with us, get in touch! Together, we can continue to celebrate and elevate African voices in literature.

2026 COMPETITION

Attention all writers of African heritage - this is your moment to shine. The 2026 Kepressng Anthology Prize will officially open for submissions on May 29, 2026. Whether you're a published author or just beginning your journey, we invite you to explore this chance to showcase your talent.

Ten lucky winners will:
~Be published in an anthology.

This year, the competition features four categories:
~ VINE
~ LILY
~ JUVENILE
~ OAK.
The theme for each category is the same as the title, but it's up to you to interpret it however you wish – literally, figuratively, or creatively.

GUIDELINES

Entry is free and open to all African and those of African descent.
~ Your work must be original, unpublished and not AI-generated.
~Your entry must be in English and fictional.
~ You can submit only one entry per category.
~ All entries must be submitted in MS Word format, double line spaced in TIMES ROMAN font.
~ Your name must not appear in the body of the story.
~ The entry must be between 5,000 and 10,000 words.
~ Your submission email title must be as follows:
CATEGORY TITLE - YOUR STORY TITLE - YOUR NAME (PSEUDONYM).
~ All entries must be received by Midday of October 11, 2026.
~ The winners will be announced six to eight weeks after the last day of submission. (A Change of date will be communicated.)

This is an incredible opportunity to have your work recognised, gain exposure, and most importantly, join a vibrant community of African writers! We can't wait to see your interpretation of these themes.

Send your submissions & FAQs to kemkaezinwo.press@gmail.com.

Good luck.

NOTES

Printed in Dunstable, United Kingdom

64898721R00119